Baby G

An Urban Tale...

Lakeya Edwards

Chris
thank you! so
much for all
the support
you Rock!.
Jessica

BABY G

This book is a _work of fiction_. Names, characters, places and incidents are products of the author's imagination or are used _fictitiously_. Any resemblance to actual events or locales or persons, living or dead is entirely coincidental. Any and all locations existing are mentioned in the book to give it a feeling of reality.

BABY G

Book Cover Model: Jessica Landon
www.facebook.com/Jessicadevillelandon

Photographer: **Natashia Burton**
nburton28@yahoo.com

Graphics Artist: **Starvin' Artist**
www.starvinartist.net

Publisher: **Baby G Entertainment, LLC**
www.BabyGLLC.com

Editing: **21st Street Urban Editing & Publishing**

www.21StreetUrbanEditing.com

Typesetting: **21st Street Urban Editing & Publishing**

www.21StreetUrbanEditing.com

BABY G

This book is dedicated to the loving memories of

Pearl Dickerson

and

Douglas G. Williams

I long to see you both again one day!

Acknowledgements

I first thank my Heavenly Father who has given me the gift of putting my thoughts and imagination to paper. I am a true witness that all things are possible through Christ Jesus. I want to thank my loving parents, Larry and Denise Edwards, for always being behind me and for giving me my first laptop that started my first novel so many years ago. Little did they know it would mean so much to me. I appreciate and love you two for all that you have done and continue to do for me and KeSean.

To my dear son, KeSean Demazio Smith, I love you more than any words that can ever be written on paper. You make Mommy want to do so much better so that you can enjoy the fruits of my labor.

To my HUGE family, the Edwards, Dickerson, Mitchell and Speight clans. I love y'all all so much and appreciate the prayers, support and all of the wonderful words of encouragement. Unfortunately, there are just too many of us to name but you all know who you are. Special shout out to all of my cousins!

To my wonderful nieces and nephews, I love you all so much and pray y'all accomplish all that you set out to do!

To my sister, Tarsha Edwards - I love you! To my other siblings - I love you all as well!

To my sister, cousin, and BFF – Andrea M. Watkins, I love and appreciate your friendship, support, unofficial editing, motivation and for always being in my corner.

To my very special aunts, Shirley and Marnetia, I love you both to pieces and appreciate our wonderful relationships.

To my BFF, Kia Coward, you are such an inspiration in every aspect of the word. I am so proud of you and appreciate everything we share. To my old BF, Mariam Boston, there is and was a season for everything and I have not forgotten the motivation, the words of encouragement, the ups and the downs, and everything we shared.

To my girls, Drea, Kia, Jessica, Laya, Stephanie, Tina, Shatarya, Quita, Kandee, Nikki, Gladys, Ebonie, Kelly, and Blue, Aisha and Kim – some of us have had our share of mishaps as well as exciting and fun times and hopefully a whole lot more memories to come. I love you all and each of you has a special place in my heart.

To the best editor in the game, Niccole Simmons, at 21st Urban Street Editing, thank you for sharing your opinion and the encouraging words. I appreciate the great work you do! I am so blessed to have come across an individual like you who believe in helping others make it in this industry.

To Azarel of Life Changing Books. I thank you for your guidance early on when I first came to you in Charlotte – it will never be forgotten.

To Karen Presley of Anointed Press Publishers. I thank you for your seminars and willingness to help. You are truly amazing!

To Natashia Burton (Photographer) and Starvin' Artist Graphic Design. You are both so talented and I appreciate the hard work you both put into my project. I look forward to a long relationship. Thank you.

To my DMV family, it is so great seeing you all at the biggest and best social gatherings and I appreciate all of the love on FB and all the social networks. I love my city!

To the WKYS and WPGC families, thank you for the support!

Special thanks to Mr. Russ Parr and Antonio the Cuban Cigar Smoker for having my back – I appreciate the continuous support!

To Shawn, thank you for being such a good father to our son and for always having positive things to say about my aspirations.

To Brian, thank you for what we shared – it was a life changing experience and the birth of something great!

To my future, I can't wait to say I do – LOL.

Last but not least, to you – my readers: I appreciate you supporting me and for all of the comments, blogs, and emails I am sure to receive. I love entertaining you and hope you enjoy this and all the other Baby G Entertainment works to follow. A hearty, THANK YOU!

If I left anyone out, charge it to my mind and definitely not my heart.

Lakeya

Chapter 1

"Layla, come down here now. Nate is at the door."

Layla's mom was always yelling about something. Whether it be the boys or her getting a job, the constant bickering and nagging was always there. Layla graduated over two months ago and since then, her mother was even more persistent with her nagging.

"Hey Nate, what's up?" Layla asked as she realized why her mother had called her and walked to the open door.

Even with her hair pinned up, she was beautiful. Layla had honey brown skin and curves in all the right places. She was definitely what a nigga would call a dime piece. Layla was the girl around the way that all the niggas were just cool with. She gambled, smoked and would straight up give a beat down for ya. She was just plain ole down to earth. What you saw with her is just what you got. For sure.

"Not a damn thing, what's poppin'?" Nate stood at the door with his blue jean shorts, a wife beater and Timbs on looking good enough to get it right there on the door stoop.

1

"There's some niggas down the street shooting that got that bread, so what's up?" Nate looked at her with a seriousness that definitely let Layla know that there was no question about these wangsta niggas that were about to feel her shot.

"I'm ready, let me just grab my bag. Mom, I'm gone, be back later." Layla locked the bottom lock and walked out the door.

Nate drove a pearl Denali fully loaded that sat on twenties and always looked as if he just drove it off the lot. As soon as they jumped in the car, Nate started running down the low on the crew that was shooting around the way. He informed Layla that they were straight up got and that they were the cousins of one of the weakest shooters around the way. All Layla could think about was the quick two or three thousand that she was about to get so she could go shopping with the girls tomorrow.

They pulled up on the block and Layla was first to jump out. She sashayed over to where the fellas were and just stood watching. The regular dudes from around the way all said what's up to her and kept shooting. But the new niggas just stood in awe and checked her out.

Sweets, who was hella sexy stood up looked behind him, saw Layla and started to laugh. "Y'all niggas wanna shoot or just stare at Layla's ass all day. She ain't nobody but our home girl."

Layla smacked her lips and rolled her eyes at Sweets before jumping in the game.

"I bet a hundred this nigga with all that damn talking he doing won't hit his point," Layla said to no one in particular.

"Damn, she fly and she shoot?" one of the dudes that Layla never seen before asked.

"Yeah, I shoot. I'm going to show you just how much once it's my turn," Layla teased.

"That's what's up. I got you on that bet," the same dude said.

It went like that for the next couple of hours until Layla broke the new dudes and got a little bit in Sweets pocket for talking smack.

"Nate, I'm hungry. What's up? Let's go to the Japanese Steak House to get something to eat," Layla said as she pushed Nate on his arm.

"Yo, that's what's up," Nate agreed and they said their goodbyes.

"Damn, Layla, that's how you rolling? You just gonna take my money and bounce?" Sweets whined.

"Nigga shut up. I ain't even get nothing from your ass for real. See y'all later. Come on Nate, let's go." Layla and Nate jumped in the truck and sped off.

"Nate, where's your CD case at? I'm tired of listening to this go-go. Put something else on." Layla complained until she got her way and Nate popped the new Jezzy CD in.

Layla just turned eighteen and was on a mission to come into her own. She rocked nothing but fly gear and kept her hair done every week. Lately, she was saving all her money to move in to her own place in Southwest, Washington, DC. Far enough from her parents in Landover, Maryland but close enough to visit whenever she felt the need. To most, Layla had it going on and always had. All her girls who coincidentally lived in DC thought she grew up with a silver spoon in her mouth but her folks worked hard to keep the roof over her head and Layla in decent clothes.

Since she was the only child, she was definitely shielded from the streets but found her way out there anyway due to the boredom she experienced living in the suburbs. Although gambling and smoking is where it started because there wasn't much else to do in her neighborhood, it definitely would not be where it stopped in her mind. She was out to have fun and she figured she only had one life to live and she was going to live it to the fullest.

They finally pulled up to the parking lot of the restaurant and Nate jumped out first while Layla sat in the truck putting more lip liner and lipstick on.

"Damn, Nate! You can't open the door for me?" she yelled as she stepped out the truck.

"You better go ahead with all that and bring your ass on here," Nate joked as he walked towards the door. He opened the door and playfully shut it and started laughing.

"You're gonna make me kick your butt if you don't stop playin'." Layla yelled as Nate reopened the door for her.

The hostess greeted them and sat them at a table where there were already three other people seated. Layla spoke and sat down. This was one of her favorite restaurants so she already knew what she wanted and didn't bother to open the menu. The waitress came over and quickly took their drink orders. Thankfully she didn't ask for ID because Layla ordered Remy straight up and the same for Nate. For Nate to be twenty-two years old he acted much older and always carried himself as such. He was one of the good guys around the way. He was who Layla first met when she moved in her neighborhood. He taught her how to shoot craps, how to set the dice and introduced her to all the fellas whom she instantly became cool with. Besides their brother-sisterly bond, Nate was also Layla's sex partner and the man she was in love with. The only problem for Layla was that he was cheap in her eyes. Sure, he would pay for them to go out whenever she wanted, or would always buy bottles and so forth at the clubs when they went. But when it came down to putting money in Layla's hand, that was not happening and Layla couldn't understand why.

The cook was now at their table putting a great show on for the child who was with the other couple at the table. He banged down his spatula which caught Layla's attention.

"Damn! He scared the hell out of me." Layla said as she grabbed her chest. Nate started laughing which caused Layla to pout and turn from him.

"Girl, go ahead. You are beyond spoiled. Aww-I'm sorry Layla boo. Want me to put a cap in that nigga for scaring you?" Nate teased.

Layla laughed and started eating the food that the cook put on her plate. She had filet mignon, chicken, shrimp, and fried rice. Nate ordered chicken, shrimp, scallops, and two orders of fried rice. With their stomachs full and three drinks later for them both, Nate paid the bill and they headed out the door.

"So, you coming with me or what?" Nate asked as they got in the truck.

"Sure, where we going?"

Nate looked at Layla with a knowing look and she grabbed her phone from her purse to call her mom and let her know that she wouldn't be home tonight. She listened to her talk about how fast she was for a few minutes before ending the call and telling her mom she loved her too. Layla loved her mom and dad but was certain she needed to find her own place as soon as possible before their relationship got worse.

"Moms still tripping? When she gonna realize that you grown?" Nate asked.

His comment caused Layla to become irritated even more and she made up her mind that she was definitely looking for a new place tomorrow. Layla shrugged and turned the music up to tune Nate out. He didn't mind. He grabbed the jay from the ashtray, lit it, hit it a couple of times and passed it to Layla.

"Here, relax Shawty. She's just worried about you and understandably so." Nate said as Layla took the jay from him, smiled and got her smoke on.

Since it was Thursday night, Layla knew that Nate was going to stop by *The Station*, the small sports bar where 'Rare Faces', a local Go-Go band played faithfully each and every Thursday. He normally came up here to meet one of his employees, as he liked to call them. Knowing he didn't have a business, Layla always laughed when she heard him use the term. Little did Layla know, hustling to Nate was a business and a very lucrative one. He had a hustle for everything. Selling shoes, phones, clothes, whatever someone would buy, he could and would sell. He had hook ups all around town and everyone was cool with him and had mad respect for his hustle. So, if they came across some goods, it was Nate they would call because they knew he would get rid of it for them.

Layla always came prepared. She grabbed her high heels out of her bag, which were red like her halter top and took the pins out of her hair to let the curls fall down. She took off her Gucci tennis shoes and threw them in the back seat. She went from being the girl around the way to a straight up diva. She touched up her lips and put a little eye shadow on. By the time she finished prepping, she looked at Nate.

"Damn, you ready? I don't understand why you going through all that. We not gonna be in here all night. I got plans for you," Nate said as he hopped out the truck. To Layla's surprise, Nate came over and opened her door.

"Since you looking like a lady, I thought I should act like a man," he said and laughed.

Layla ignored his comment and switched to the door of the club. The bouncer at the door immediately opened the door for Layla and greeted them both. "Hey Sexy. What's up Nate?" he said as he gave Nate dap.

Nate looked around as if he was looking for someone. "Hey Moe, what's up? Where you see someone sexy at?" Nate joked.

"Don't hate, Nate." Layla winked at Moe and walked through the door, rolling her eyes at Nate.

Once in, Layla walked straight to the bathroom. It was small as hell with only two stalls and a large mirror. Layla walked straight over to the mirror to see how she looked.

"Hey Layla, what's going on?" Layla turned around to see a friend of hers name Lyn that she was once really tight with. Lyn grew up in the same neighborhood with Layla but she started being the neighborhood hoe and Layla slowly allowed their relationship to go sour.

"Hey Lyn, how you been?"

"I'm good girl. I thought I would come out since my mom babysitting and get my freak on," Lyn laughed.

Layla laughed with her but knew she literally meant just what she said. She was sure she was going to leave with someone tonight. Layla had to admit that Lyn still looked good after having two kids at such a young age. If she carried herself as good as she looked, she would probably still be Layla's home girl. Layla had tried talking sense into Lyn plenty of times and even took her

8

to church with her and her parents but Lyn was just set in her ways and thought sexing every guy she met was going to bring her stability. Layla loved sex just as much as the next person but she knew her body was her temple and so she tried to treat it as such. Though – still very cordial Layla would always have her back regardless. And Layla was sure Lyn felt the same way. After making sure she looked good, she gave Lyn a hug and told her she would see her out there and left Lyn in the mirror putting her lipstick on. As soon as Layla walked out, she saw Nate talking to Nut who was one of Nate's workers and walked in their direction. She was stopped by three different guys on the way over asking her if she wanted a drink. She declined and approached Nate and Nut.

"What's up, Nut? You looking fresh as always."

"I'm just trying to keep up with y'all," he said before giving Layla a hug.

Nate handed Layla a drink and smiled.

"See you gonna have me all twisted and what not?" Layla questioned while taking the drink. Layla moved a little in front of them so she wouldn't be all up in their business. The band members were all assembling on the stage which indicated they were about to start playing.

"What's up DC, Maryland, and VA? We appreciate y'all coming to support us each and every Thursday here at *The Station* and don't forget to come and see us each and every Saturday at *Club Winds*. Ladies free before eleven and fellas twenty dollars before midnight. Y'all ready to party?" This was the lead male rapper of the group getting the crowd ready for the show.

They started off mellow, singing; *I'm a Flirt*, by R. Kelly. After which, they started rocking. Layla was in her own world and feeling her drinks. She started grinding and swaying her hips from side to side. She was putting on a serious show for the guys who were mesmerized by her seductive movements. Nate laughed to himself and just knew she was in for a hell of a night. After he finished conducting business, he went behind Layla and just stood. She caught the drift and started giving him a show and dancing all around him. It went like that for the next hour before Nate had enough and decided to bounce.

Chapter 2

"Layla, get your drunk ass up and in the house. I refuse to carry you up those steps. You shouldn't drink so much if you can't handle it."

Nate was irritated that Layla let herself get so twisted and instantly fell asleep as soon as they got in the truck.

"I'm good. Stop yelling. Dang." Layla whined and got out the truck.

Her hair was all over her head but she still managed to look good. Nate looked at her and hoped she wasn't too twisted to give him some. Nate had a cozy apartment in Greenbelt, Maryland where he rarely stayed. He still had a room at his parent's house in their basement in Landover and normally crashed there instead of taking the fifteen minute drive to his apartment. Nate was a neat freak so he demanded that everyone take their shoes off when they came in his apartment. His carpet was beige and free of stains. When you walked in, there was a long hallway with the coat closet and at the end of the hallway there was the guest bathroom and the dining room to the right. He had a really nice glass dining room table with black sculpture dolphins in the center holding the glass top and a really nice floral arrangement in black and gold which were the colors of the rest of the living room. There were gold mini blinds in the living room and a black leather sectional couch with an identical cocktail table with dolphins that sat in the middle of the sectional. The sectional was swallowed with gold pillows that really set it off. To say the least, Nate's place was off the chain nice. Layla went straight to the bathroom to take a shower and make sure she was presentable. She knew that the one thing Nate hated was to see her not handling her liquor. After taking a shower, she pulled out her toothbrush from her bag and brushed her teeth.

"Get it together girl. Go show him what's up." Layla stayed in the bathroom another five minutes talking herself into a sober state and then walked out the bathroom and into the living room where Nate sat watching an old boxing match on HBO.

"You alright?" he asked. He picked up the remote from the cocktail table and gave Layla a look of disgust.

"Yeah, I'm good. What you looking at?"

Layla walked over to the couch and kneeled between Nate's legs. She grabbed his neck and started kissing him. He started to say something but Layla put her finger over his mouth and told him to be quiet. She then got up and turned the stereo on to Ledisi's new album and turned the television off. The only lights were the lights from the stereo player. She walked back over to Nate and stripped naked and kneeled back between his legs. Nate was just sitting and watching her trying not to say a word. His dick spoke for him since it was sticking straight up looking like it was about to pop out of his shorts. Layla unbuttoned his shorts and pulled them and his boxers down to his ankles. She slowly took him in her mouth teasing him with her tongue. She knew how to please Nate and knew he loved her to make slurping noises when she sucked him. So, she did just that. She teased and sucked Nate for about forty-five minutes making sure to ease up when it felt and looked as if he was about to cum. Nate lifted her up in his arms and walked toward the bedroom trying to untangle his pants and boxers from around his ankles. Finally free, he laid Layla on the bed and went straight for her love button. He licked Layla until she couldn't take anymore and she begged him to put it in. Nate quickly grabbed a condom from his nightstand and began kissing Layla before slowly entering her.

"Oh, Nate. Yes, Baby!" Nate continued to move to the rhythm of Layla's body until he couldn't take it anymore.

"Damn, Layla. I'm about to cum," he screamed.

"So am I, Baby. Don't stop, Boo," was all Layla could get out before she started to cum with Nate. Nate collapsed on Layla before she pushed him off to go wash up. When she came back, Nate was knocked out. She took the condom off him, threw it away, and washed him off before getting back in the bed with him. It didn't take her any time before falling asleep.

Layla woke up before Nate so she took a shower and went to see if anything was in his kitchen to cook. Since Nate rarely stayed there, he didn't have anything worth cooking for breakfast. She walked back into his room and woke him up.

"Nate, wake up. I'm hungry. Plus I am meeting Monique and Yve today. Wake up."

Nate finally started coming to and jumped up to see what time it was. It was eleven o'clock.

"Damn, Layla. Why you let me sleep so late? I was supposed to get a haircut and meet Lil Ray at noon. Damn, I won't be able to get my hair cut. Come on, I'm getting dressed over my moms. Grab your things and let's roll."

They both slipped on their clothes and headed out the door. Layla convinced Nate to stop at *White Corners,* which was a nice Korean owned breakfast shop near their neighborhood where all the around the way non-working guys hung out and chilled. She ran in and ordered her and Nate a breakfast sandwich. While waiting, she could see Nate in the truck looking irritated and on the phone running off at the mouth to God only knew who.

"What's up, cutie? Ain't it too early for you to be looking that good?"

Layla turned around to see a nice looking guy with a *Hermano* sweat suit on and the new black Jordan's to match. She smiled, and turned around to the Korean lady bagging her food and waiting for the money. Before she could reach in her bag, the dude from behind her gave the lady a twenty.

"Somebody as fine as you shouldn't ever have to pay for anything. I'm Malachi," he said while extending his hand.

"I'm Layla, and someone as cocky as you doesn't seem like the type to buy another man's food. But, I'm certain he would say thank you."

Layla grabbed the bag and strutted out the door. She jumped in the truck and Nate sped off. As bad as she wanted to look back, she didn't.

Malachi was stuck looking out the door and wondering how he just got carried by someone so beautiful. He definitely was going to find out who she was and make sure she knew just who he was. The rejection kind of turned him on and he probably would have cussed her ass out had he been around anyone other than the clowns in the store. He laughed it off and placed his order.

Layla gave Nate a goodbye kiss and ran into the house and straight to her room which was also in her parent's basement. It allowed her to have the luxury of her own private room, bathroom, and mini sitting area where her and her girls could chill without being interrupted by her folks. As soon as she entered her room, she turned her cell phone on and placed it on the charger. She noticed she had four new messages. She grabbed her house phone and checked her messages. Two were from Yve and one from Monique. Both were calling to make sure they were still hooking up today. The last message was from this dude name Al who Layla shoots with from time to time. He was calling to see if she was coming through the park today. She deleted the messages and called Monique.

"Hey Girl, what's up?" Monique answered.

Monique and Layla had been friends for a couple of years and met during the brief time in which Layla's dad and mom split up and Layla attended a DC junior high school. They quickly bonded and became best friends.

"Ain't nothing. About to jump in the shower. What time are you coming to get me?" Layla gathered her things for her shower while waiting for Monique to respond.

"Girl, your ass was about to get left. I just picked Yve up and we about to spark a fat one," Monique said.

"We're not waiting around all day for her. I put something on hold the other day, and I want to get it before someone else does," Yve shouted through the phone.

"Tell her to stop whining and I will be ready by the time y'all get here. Plus I need you to run me pass *The View Condos* to fill out an application before we hit the mall. They are leasing now."

Layla hung up and rushed to take her shower and get dressed. She dressed in a pair of Rock & Republic tapered jeans, a cute low cut white and gold Prada tank top, and Jimmy Choo gold sandals to match. She grabbed her cell phone off the charger and dropped it in her bag. Layla then ran upstairs to use her mom's Bvlgari perfume since nothing was left in her own bottle. While upstairs, her parent's phone was ringing. She didn't even think twice about answering. She figured it wasn't for her so she went in the kitchen and fixed her a glass of ice and grabbed a drink. She thought she heard her phone ringing downstairs but refused to go back down and answer it. She went to the front door and opened it knowing that it must have been Monique and Yve who was calling her. To her surprise they weren't there yet so she went back to the living room and turned the television on. Her cell phone was ringing and after digging in her bag, she finally found it.

Irritated, she answered. "Hello?" she said with a slight hint of disgust.

"Layla, why are you not answering the phones in the house? I called your line and mine." It was Layla's mom.

"Oh, I'm sorry mommy. I didn't hear my phone and just knew yours wasn't for me."

"Obviously you knew wrong." Layla's mom said.

All Layla could do was laugh because her mother was always getting smart with someone. She was at work and asked Layla to take out the turkey wings from the freezer and sit them in the sink for her to cook when she got off. Layla did what she was asked and then heard her friends blowing the horn out front.

"Alright mom, I'm about to go to the mall with Monique and Yve so I will see you later."

"I'm going to church tonight if y'all want to go with me." Layla's mom suggested.

"On a Friday, no thanks. We good."

"Suppose the Lord said that every time you asked Him for something? He probably would say, on a Sunday, no I'm good too," Layla's mom joked.

"Aww-go ahead Ma. I'm about to leave. Love you and see you later."

"Okay, Love you too and y'all be safe. Tell Monique and Yve I said hello and that I want to see them both in church on Sunday."

"No doubt, bye Mom." Layla hung up and rushed out to the car.

Layla, Monique, and Yve had just left from filling out Layla's application at what Layla hoped would be her new home in Southwest, Washington, DC. Nate had actually mentioned the luxury condos to Layla a couple months ago and told her she needed to go fill out an application and that the girl would look out for her. At the time, Layla was too busy shopping and having fun since she had just graduated high school and wanted all her money to herself instead of worrying about the future. But, now that her folks were on her case, Layla knew she had to make a move. So, she went and filled out the application and to her surprise, the girl named Cookie who Nate had told her to ask for a while back was still there and she did just what Nate said she would do. She skipped the portion concerning where she worked and all and just told her she would handle it for a small fee. Layla wasn't surprised, she figured everybody had to have a hustle, so she chalked it up and gave the lady three extra hundred dollars in addition to the two-hundred and fifty dollar security deposit. Layla was sure she would have to start saving up her money if she was going to pay a thirteen hundred dollar bill every month.

"Layla, where were you last night?" Yve, asked as they were walking into *Tyson's Corner Mall*.

"Dang, nosey. I was chillin'. Why, did you miss me?"

"Girl, please. Miss you, hell no! If anything your ass missed me. I was with Jayden last night. But, I did call you and was just wondering why your phone was off. Don't get it twisted, I ain't no carpet muncher." Yve said and bumped pass Layla to hurry to get through the door of Saks.

"Look, don't start with me. Monique, you better get your girl."

They all laughed and walked into the store. It always shocked Layla how all three clicked like they been friends for years. But in actuality, Monique and Yve had only been friends about two years and had met through Layla. Layla met Yve when she hung out around her cousin Mia's way growing up. Her cousin Mia lived in the heart of Southeast and Layla use to be pressed just to go spend the night and get a little of the ghetto action. Her parents really weren't down for her spending so much time around Mia because they considered her too old and too fast for Layla. If they stuck with that, Layla might still have her virginity. But, as much as she loves good loving, doubt it very seriously. She figured she still would have met Nate and that would be that. Yve was actually Mia's friend and they all hung out whenever she would visit. So, the two clicked and when Mia got arrested for stabbing a girl around her way, it was Yve who helped her fight and hid the knife afterwards which caused Mia's sentence to get dropped considerably. So, Layla had love for Yve for that reason and they grew extremely close while Mia was locked up. Mia came home and turned her life completely around. She eventually got married and only hangs out with them on rare occasions.

Yve was glad to find out that the *Chloé* dress she put on hold was still there. So, Yve left with her dress, which set her back fifteen hundred dollars, a pair of *Jimmy Choo* pumps, and a *Louis Vuitton* satchel. Monique had a bag full of clothes from *BEBE* and a cute *BCBG* colorful keyhole dress. While Layla brought a fifteen hundred dollar *Chanel* bag and a dress from *Neiman's*. The girls made plans to get appetizers from *Ruth Chris Steakhouse* downtown on 9th Street and then hit, *The Love Night Club,* that night. Monique dropped them off and promised to be back by nine o'clock to pick them up.

Chapter 3

As soon as Monique walked into her apartment, she put her bags down and started counting how much money she had left. She had left her house that morning with two thousand dollars and still had eleven hundred dollars left. Monique was the frugal one of the three. She worked hard for her money and made sure she always had something to fall back on. Monique made at least four hundred dollars a day braiding hair. She was the best individual braiding female in the DC Metropolitan area and the best part was that it only took her three to four hours to complete. That was record breaking for those plaits and what kept her clientele full and coming back.

Monique was five-nine, weighed one hundred twenty pounds, and could have easily been a model. She was light brown with big bright eyes and a hair full of thick jet black hair that she kept mostly in a cute bushy ponytail due to the time she felt it took to do her own hair. Although she was thin, she had big breast. Monique had her own place since she was seventeen years old. Her father died when she was young during a drug bust in the early eighties and her mother was in St. Elizabeth mental institution because she often suffered from nervous breakdowns. Monique was determined to stay out of the system, even if it was only for a year. She talked her mom into voluntarily admitting herself before the authorities were called and she kept their apartment in Southeast. Monique made it a habit to visit her mom at least twice a week and take her home cooked meals on each visit. Even though Monique was not big on attending church, she prayed faithfully for her mother's healing. She knew her mom missed her father dearly and even respected the love she held for him but it was times when she couldn't understand why her mom wouldn't get better for her, her only child.

Monique kept her apartment up nicely. She redecorated the entire apartment in her favorite color, silver. Monique was extremely talented and so creative that she painted her mother's green leather couch to grey and if she didn't tell anyone, you could never have noticed. She showed you that with the right kind of spray paint, you can make anything happen. It was six o'clock and Monique decided to take a nap before having to get dressed. She took off all her clothes, except her undergarments and grabbed the roach out the ashtray in front of her to finish off the rest.

Monique's cell phone started ringing, so she got up from the couch and went over to the kitchen table where her purse was sitting. She finally found it and pushed talk before it went to her voicemail. She immediately recognized the number. It was this dude she recently met named Carlos.

"Hello?"

"Hey Monique, this Carlos what you doing?"

She immediately went back to the couch to lie down and talk. "Oh, nothing. Just got in here from the mall. What you up to?"

"I'm chillin'. What you get me? I know you ain't go to the mall without buying your new boo something, right?"

Monique smiled and was glad he asked. "Oh, you know I don't know what your taste is like, but we can certainly go out together the next time so I can be sure to get something you like," she said while trying not to laugh.

Carlos was impressed. He thought she would get smart and that would've let him know exactly the type of chick he was dealing with.

"That's what's up. We can do that tomorrow if you want. But what you getting into tonight? I'm trying to take you out."

"Oh, me and my girls are supposed to be going to Ruth Chris and then to *The Love* around nine. So, tonight might not be good. Do you go to clubs? If so, you are always welcome to meet us at *The Love*." Monique extended the invitation knowing that if Carlos accepted, he would be buying her and her girls drinks all night.

"Ain't Raheim Devaughn performing up there tonight?" Carlos asked.

"That's right, he is. We didn't even think about that when we decided to go there tonight. That's even better. So, you coming through or what?" Monique asked.

"Yeah, me and my man might slide through. If we do, I will see you there, otherwise, I'm still trying to grab something to eat and maybe slide to Georgetown to see what kind of taste you have," Carlos said and started laughing.

"Okay, that's a bet. Since you haven't seen me since getting my number, I will be wearing a pink dress and silver sandals."

"Sweetie, it wouldn't matter what you wear; I couldn't forget that pretty face. I'll see you later or if not, definitely tomorrow. Be safe and don't party too hard. I can't have my future wife acting up." Carlos didn't give Monique a chance to respond before hanging up.

Monique sat on the couch thinking of Carlos and his comment. She eventually dozed off.

When Yve arrived in the house, she went straight upstairs and ran a hot bath. Yve had a really nice new town home in Southeast, which was recently built and purchased for her by her last boyfriend. Instead of working hard, Yve depended on the guys in her life to do for her. There was Jayden who was as close to a boyfriend as she had. He paid her mortgage every month but her only complaint was that he required too much of her time. Yve was great at manipulating people and so that's what she did. She could talk someone that she just met into buying her anything she wanted. She just had the gift of gab like that.

Yve grew up with her grandmother who had recently relocated to Charlotte, North Carolina where their family was originally from. Her grandmother had been trying unsuccessfully to get her to visit for the last year.

Unlike Layla and Monique, Yve had very light skin. She had grey eyes and wore her hair short like Halle Berry. It fit her perfect. Although both her parents were black, she was always asked if she was mixed. She was very good looking and for some reason only attracted ballers.

When her money was low and she didn't want to ask one of her many friends for funds, she would do photo shoots for different promoters in the city and premiere on most of the top party fliers. It paid well and she enjoyed playing model.

Yve grabbed her iPod and put it in the Bose speakers. She set it to shuffle through her list of songs, grabbed candles from the linen closet and headed to the bathroom. On her way to the bathroom, her doorbell rang. Yve grabbed her robe from the back of the bathroom door and headed downstairs to open the door.

"What's up, boo?"

Yve looked at Jayden with darts in her eyes. "How many times do I have to tell you not to pop up over my house?" Yve put her hand on her hip and waited for a response.

"Girl, you gonna let me in or make me stand out here," was Jayden response.

Yve moved to the side to let him in.

"I was just about to get in the tub. It's girls night out so Monique will be coming to get me shortly."

She turned around and started walking back upstairs towards the bathroom.

Jayden was right on her heels. "Where y'all going?"

"Jayden, do I question you about where you go and with whom? We are not in a relationship so you need to chill out with all those damn questions."

"Oh, yeah? That ain't what the hell you say when I kick out that dough every damn month."

"Whatever, Jayden." Yve brushed Jayden off, took her robe off and got in the tub

"Damn, boo. You want some company?"

"Not really honey, I want to relax. What brings you by?" Yve relaxed in the tub and looked over at Jayden who was sitting on the toilet.

"I was coming to see if you wanted to go to dinner or something but you always so busy."

"Why didn't you call?"

"I did, but your phone went straight to voicemail." Jayden got up and walked to the tub. He grabbed Yve's washcloth, lathered it up, and started washing her up.

He started with her legs and worked up to her thighs which caused her to let out a moan. Jayden put the washcloth between her legs and gently rubbed her sensitive spot.

"Damn, boo. I guess you really don't want me to go out, huh?" Yve was getting excited and started contemplating telling the girls she would catch them the next time but didn't want to hear Layla's mouth.

"That would be nice. We can go grab something to eat and catch a movie. I'm trying to see that new *Planet of the Apes* movie that just came out."

"Baby, I tell you what, we can spend the day together tomorrow. I don't want to let them down because we been planning to go out tonight for a while. But, what you can do is make your Yve feel real good before she goes out and that way, you will be on her mind from the time she leave, until the time she comes back?"

Jayden continued to wash Yve up and contemplated what she had said. He then asked her to stand up and he turned the shower on to rinse her off. He grabbed her towel, put it around her, and picked her up. He then walked her to her bedroom and laid her on the bed.

Jayden grabbed the lotion from the dresser and rubbed it all on Yve's body. Yve was getting seriously turned on and extremely wet. In anticipation, she took the lotion from him and quickly took control. She began taking his clothes off starting with his shoes and then worked her way up careful to put his clothes on the ottoman at the foot of the bed knowing that he hated his clothes to be wrinkled. Plus she didn't know whether he was going out afterwards.

Yve knew she needed to get dressed soon and have enough time to take a quick shower before leaving so she pushed Jayden on the bed and straddled him. She grabbed all nine inches of him and led him inside her. Jayden was enjoying every minute and didn't mind that she obviously intended for it to be a quickie. Yve was riding Jayden and licking his nipples at the same time. She then stopped and asked Jayden to enter her from behind in which he eagerly obliged. While he was hitting Yve from the back, Yve was playing with her spot and steady building up her orgasm.

"Damn Yve, I can't hold it any longer. I'm cumming boo," Jayden said as he squirted his cum all over Yve's ass.

"Baby," Yve was now whining and about to get upset that she didn't cum. But before she could, Jayden slapped her ass, grabbed her towel from the floor and wiped her off. He then turned her around and started eating her out. Yve felt like she was in heaven it felt so good. As he licked her spot, she played with her nipples which was turning Jayden back on.

"Right there, boo. Lick it, baby." Yve was gyrating her hips to Jayden's tongue movement. She grabbed his head and held on tight because she was exploding.

"Yes, yes, yes! That's what's up, Boo."

Yve jumped up, gave Jayden a kiss and ran in the bathroom to take a shower.

"Dang, Yve. That's how you going? I want some more." Yve was ignoring him. She was satisfied and ready to get her party on.

The girls pulled up to *Ruth Chris* and parked valet. Monique's gold 745 Beamer was sparkling and the girls looked great. Layla had on a short black Versace dress that she bought the previous week with red pumps and her red Chanel bag to match. While Yve was a little more casual with Seven jean capris, a gold tube top, and gold strap sandals. Monique wore her pink BEBE dress with spaghetti straps, silver sandals, and a silver clutch. The girls were fearless and strutted into *Ruth Chris*. *Ruth Chris* was an upscale restaurant; it attracted only the money makers in town and very rarely was ever overly crowded.

Layla was the first to reach the lounge area. There was a piano player to the right of the room near the window with high cocktail tables surrounding it and a long mahogany bar with four forty-two-inch plasma televisions located overhead where sports and news normally aired. Layla headed straight to the bar and ordered a Ciroc on the rocks, a Remy Side Car for Yve, and a Margarita for Monique. Monique and Yve left Layla to get their drinks and went to the restroom. When they returned, Layla was sitting at the bar engaged in conversation with a man who looked old enough to be Layla's grandfather. Monique and Yve introduced themselves and sat down a couple of seats away.

"Dang, he's old." Yve said to Monique after taking a sip of her drink.

"You know Layla don't care. She will let them wine and dine her and not give them so much as a kiss. But they the dumb ones. So, if I was her, I would play their ass too." Monique said and raised her glass to Layla.

Layla saw the gesture and raised hers as well. The man who Yve and Monique later found out name was Maurice, told them to order whatever they wanted and it would be on him. He asked them to call him Moe. The girls didn't hold back a little bit. They came for appetizers and ended up ordering full course meals. By the time they finished ordering drinks, and dinner, their bill came up to six hundred dollars. Layla and the girls thanked Moe, Layla gave him her number, and they left to head to the club. It was just like Layla to meet someone that always ended up paying their entire bill. So, the girls were getting hyped.

After waiting for the valet, the girls got in the car. The girls were feeling nice and so they turned up the music loud and started singing with Beyoncé's, *Countdown*. They sang loud enough for whoever was around to hear them shouting. Layla didn't waste any time and started rolling a jay.

"Did y'all know that Raheim is going to be up at *Love* tonight?"

"Monique you late, we told you that about a month ago. You know Demazio is going to hook us up with VIP." Yve said as she took the jay from Layla.

Demazio was Yve's ex-boyfriend and the owner of *The Love.*

"Layla, call Nate and see if him and Delonté are coming to the club. Maybe he can bring that fire with him," Monique said and took the jay from Yve.

"I talked to him before I left out the house, he said he was coming through but he didn't say who would be with him. Delonté is not thinking about your butt," Layla said and gave Monique a smirk.

Yve was in the back and quiet as could be.

"Yve, are you okay?" Monique turned around to see what Yve was doing.

"Girl, I'm fine. You better keep your eyes on the road." Yve said, after she snapped out of the stuck mode she was in.

The girls were quiet and in their own world the rest of the ride.

BABY G

Chapter 4

When they pulled in the front of the club. The valet took their keys and the ladies all stepped out the car as if they were on the red carpet. To be honest, they all definitely looked like they needed to be.

The bouncer at the front door noticed Yve and her girlfriends as soon as they stepped out the car. He told the guy at the bottom of the steps that checked ID's to let them through. The girls all thanked him and gave him a kiss on the check because the line was wrapped around the corner and it probably would have taken an hour to get Demazio on the phone to come out and get them. Demazio and Yve broke up because Yve was tired of not getting that much time with him. Demazio was too busy building his empire. Their intimate relationship grew apart but they remained good friends and talked at least twice a week.

Yve, knowing the game, slid the bouncer a fifty dollar bill and gave him a wink. Once inside, the ladies couldn't get in the door good before guys were coming at them. They decided to walk around and check out the scenery before getting a drink. Their drinks from earlier and the bud they smoked had them where they wanted to be for the moment. The club was decorated mostly in burnt orange and brown. There were plush leather burnt orange chairs and couches throughout the main level where the entrance was and brown leather post that resembled stripper pole's by every couch. In the middle of the room sat a huge square bar that housed bartenders in all white instead of the normal black that most wear. Demazio made sure that the female bartenders were gorgeous. They all looked good enough to be top models and that included the male bartenders as well. The club was definitely plush and fit for only the best. It was a little before midnight and the club was already packed. Raheim was going to be performing soon so the girls decided to head to the VIP room to see who was hanging out tonight. On any given night, you could easily find some of the hottest celebrities that were in town. From the Wizard players like Rashard Lewis and John Wall to former Nugget players like Carmelo Anthony and DerMarr 'Slim' Johnson, to Ciara and P. Diddy. It was nothing to see a celebrity chilling in the VIP lounge of *The Love*. When the girls walked to the door, none of them were paying attention to the guy guarding the door. Yve walked directly up to him.

"Hello. My girls and I were on our way to see what was poppin' in the VIP room. Are you the gentleman running things?" she said as seductively as possible.

"Yeah, that would be me." he looked Yve up and down as if he was not impressed at all.

"Oh, well since you running things, could you get on that little walkie-talkie and tell Demazio that Yve is in front of you and need access to the VIP area." She was trying not to get irritated with the guy who she thought had to be new because she hadn't seen him before now. He quickly wiped the inferior look off his face and radioed Demazio.

"Yo, Demazio, come in. I got a young lady up here by the name of Yve who want access. She got two other ladies with her."

"Yeah, they good. Give them a band and tell them to order what they want and I will be up there shortly."

He snapped a yellow band on each of their arms and Yve couldn't help but to now act like her shit didn't stink. It took everything out of her not to stick her tongue out at him.

When the girls walked into the VIP area which was located on the upper level, they headed to the bar. The VIP area took up the entire upper level of the club and had a large balcony that overlooked the main level of the club. Raheim was performing on the main level stage so it would be perfect for those that didn't want to deal with the crowd below. The bar was lined against the wall around the entire room. The couches were chocolate brown leather with big throw pillows. The carpet was a gold-mustard color and there were two gold pool tables in the center of the room. All of the flutes and champagne glasses that hung over the bar were all trimmed in gold. The VIP room definitely lived up to its name. The girls weren't at the bar for five minutes before Anton, Demazio's right hand man walked over to them.

"Damn, ladies. Y'all looking good tonight." Anton, commented while giving the girls a hug and kiss.

"Thank you, Anton." Layla was the first to speak.

Anton had been trying to get with Layla for a while but she wouldn't budge. They went out a couple of times but nothing ever came of it. Truth be told, Layla was only into Nate at the time to give someone else the time of day.

"Layla, what's up? When we going out again?"

"Whenever you get rid of all your groupies. Which I'm sure will be never," Layla responded.

"Whatever. You know those rats don't mean nothing to me. Come over on the other side. We got a table set up. Plus, I want you ladies to meet Raheim."

They all walked to the other side of the room where Raheim and his mini entourage were sitting. He was very polite and got up to give each of them hugs. Layla was thinking how short he looked compared to his videos. But although he was short, he was still handsome. She couldn't wait to hear him serenade the crowd.

Anton left the ladies to mingle with Raheim and his friends and went to handle business. After about ten minutes, Demazio walked in with Nate and his friend Delonté. Nate had on dark blue True Religion jeans, a dark green Ed Hardy shirt, Ed Hardy tennis shoes, and a dark green Ed Hardy hat to match. He was looking damn good. Delonté was not to be out done because he too looked good with his Sabiado short set on and LeBron

James tennis shoes. Nate and Demazio stepped off in the direction of the bar and were talking about what Layla assumed to be business. Delonté walked over to where the girls were at. He first gave Raheim dap and a brotherly hug and then gave all the girls a hug.

"What's up, Monique. You trying to hit this with me?" Delonté pulled a jay from his sweat suit pocket. Monique took it from him, took a lighter out her purse, and lit it. By this time, the VIP room was getting extremely crowded. They heard the DJ announce that Raheim would be taking the stage in ten minutes. Raheim got up with his mini entourage and walked down to the main level. Layla and Yve walked over to the bar where Demazio and Nate were at.

"Damn, you wasn't going to come over and speak" Layla stood in front of Nate with her hand on her hip.

"Layla go ahead. I was just talking business. I was about to come over there. Where Delonté at?" Nate tried giving Layla a hug but she tried to resist but easily gave in when he kissed her on her neck.

"They on the other side of the room, smoking and talking."

Just then, the waitress came over, and whispered something in Nate's ear. Layla was taken aback. All she thought was that this heffa is straight disrespecting.

"Excuse me. Did you not just see us talking? Damn, you rude." Layla moved close to the girl which caused the girl to step back.

"Layla, stop tripping." Nate turned to the girl, gave her five hundred dollar bills, and asked her to bring them a couple of bottles of Moët.

Raheim started performing and the crowd got hyped. DC was definitely feeling him.

The cocktail waitress brought back four bottles of Moët and Nate whispered in her ear to keep the change. Layla immediately looked at him and rolled her eyes.

"Shawty, you know what? I'm going to start calling you Baby G. Yo, D and Yve—Layla's new name now is Baby G." Layla looked at Nate and rolled her eyes again. Monique was the first to speak.

"Aww, that's cute, Baby Girl. Zo, you remember when we had our little pet names for each other."

Nate was laughing and pulling on Layla. "Naw, it's not Baby Girl. It's Baby Gangsta. 'Cause shawty here is just thorough. This here is my Baby Gangsta."

Layla couldn't help but laugh. "You can call me what you want but if I see her whispering in your ear again, you gonna be calling the police," Layla said and grabbed Yve's arm, a bottle of Moët, and walked back to the other side of the room.

"I see what you mean, Nate. Layla is really not to be messed with. But, on the real, when y'all gonna make things official and be a couple?"

Nate looked over at Layla and smiled. "As soon as I finish stacking this paper, that's my word. Shit, your ass set the bar so damn high by buying Yve a damn house and a Lexus." The two of them slap hands and shared a nice laugh together.

"True, I feel you, Dog. You know they got to be treated like the queens they are."

"No doubt," Nate responded.

Demazio stood up and told Nate he had to go check on the club.

"Layla, do you see who just walked up in this joint?" Monique moved closer to Layla so she wouldn't be overheard by Delonté. The last thing she needed was for Delonté to think she was being disrespectful.

"Who girl? All I can see is the crowd of people. Whoever it is, they got like twenty people with them. All that is not necessary," Layla said unimpressed by the entourage.

Just as Monique was about to tell her, Layla saw the dude that she had seen earlier that day in White Corners. "Oh, let me find out."

"Let you find out what?" Monique said to Layla and turned in the direction of Layla's eyes.

"Ain't that the dude who owns that clothing store uptown? What's his name?" Monique was hitting Layla's leg trying to remember the dude's name.

"Malachi."

"Yeah, Malachi. You know him? He owns that store, Hermano. His store is on fire right now. All the big time hustlers and big names be wearing his shit. From what I hear, he supposed to go mainstream."

Layla had tuned Monique out and wasn't interested in all that. "Come on y'all. Let's go mingle downstairs."

She was not trying to run into Mr. Cocky again. However, as luck would have it, as soon as she stood up, Malachi saw her. It was hard not to notice three of the most beautiful women in the room. He immediately recognized her as the girl from earlier that day who carried him. He watched as they headed for the door and saw as Layla whispered something in Nate's ear at the bar.

Yo, Levi – that's the chick that was at White Corner's yesterday I was telling you 'bout." Malachi was looking so hard at Layla that you could have sworn he could see through her clothes.

"Which one? It's like two hundred women up in this piece." Levi was Malachi's brother and they were as close as two men could possibly be. They did everything together, including business. They were partners in their clothing line, Hermano, which meant brother in Spanish. The two were inseparable.

"The shawty in the black and red. Do you see her, she's walking out now." Levi was looking over Malachi's shoulder and spotted Layla and her two girlfriends walking out the door.

"Yeah, I see her. She's nice and shawty look familiar as hell. I wanna know who the cute red bone is. Honey got it going on, for sure."

Malachi nudged his brother to follow him downstairs. They left the folks they were with and the only reason for them being there. Neither really liked to party like that, but their main man, Dre, was celebrating his engagement so they couldn't miss it even if they wanted to.

As soon as Malachi and Levi walked out of the VIP area, women were on them hard. While Levi was enjoying the attention, Malachi was on a mission to find Layla. He saw the three women close to the stage enjoying the end of Raheim's performance. He walked behind Layla and seductively whispered into her ear.

"Funny seeing you here."

He scared Layla because vibes from his baritone voice in her ear was unexpected so she jumped a little and quickly turned around as the chills made the hairs on her neck stiffen.

"Damn Baby, I don't bite. Why you jumping?"

Layla smiled and turned back around. Monique saw the exchange between the two and quickly jumped in. She held her hand out and introduced herself and Yve, and then told him Layla's name. Malachi shook both their hands, turned around to see where Levi was, made eye contact with him, and waved his hand to come over to where he was. When he came over, Malachi first introduced Yve and then Monique. He introduced Layla last.

"Levi, this here is Ms. Layla. She kind of mean though."

Layla was busy clapping at Raheim's performance and barely hearing what Malachi was saying. She turned around after he thanked the audience. "I'm sorry. I just really wanted to hear the end of that song."

She extended her hand to Levi. Levi shook hers and it clicked as to where he heard her name and saw her before.

"Hey, I think I met you before. You that shawty that got that mean shot that the fellas uptown be talking about. I think I saw you around Trinidad with some dude in a white truck."

Layla was amused and thought she would play with him for a minute. "I'm sorry, shoot. I don't shoot guns. Never even held one in my life." She looked at Monique and Yve, and the girls burst out laughing.

"Oh, you had me there for a minute." Levi looked at Yve and asked her if she wanted to go to the bar to get a round of drinks for everyone. She thought he was cute with his sexy smile and dimples – not to mention he was rocking a Cartier watch laced with emerald diamonds that lay lavishly on his wrist, so of course she decided to go with him. She asked Monique and Layla what they wanted and the two walked off.

Monique excused herself to the ladies room to give the two a little privacy. Malachi was stuck looking at Layla with his baby brown eyes and she was about to say something when he interrupted her.

"So, you shoot craps, huh? You don't look like the type to be on the ground grinding like that." Malachi said while looking directly in Layla's eyes. Layla turned away for a mere second. She was seriously tripping off of how attracted she was to him. Malachi was definitely handsome, and he definitely was representing his clothing line well. He had on a black jacket with his label name in funny letters scattered on the back, some jeans, which she figured was also by his company, a white Hermano polo t-shirt, and black *Prada* loafers. She sized him up and was feeling his style. Unlike his brother, he didn't wear much jewelry. However, she noticed that he had on a ring.

"Yeah, I shoot from time to time."

"Now that's funny." Malachi started laughing.

This caused Layla to become offended. "What's funny," Layla said, and put her hand her on hip.

"It's funny that you shoot craps, you running game like that? I bet you live somewhere in the suburbs or something."

"Excuse, me? First of all. I don't just shoot craps, I break niggas that think they got game. And second of all, I must not be that much of a joke since your brother obviously knows my stats. You know what, I'm not even sure why I am standing here entertaining you." Malachi was still laughing at Layla and it caused her to really get upset.

"It was nice meeting you, umm. What's your name again." This caused Malachi to stop laughing.

"You're joking, right?"

"No, I'm not. Anyway, I'm going to get my girls because I think it's time to call it a night."

Layla walked off towards the direction that Levi and Yve had walked in and once again, left Malachi standing by himself trying to figure out how he got carried. Layla found the girls, sent a message to Nate's side kick letting him know she was leaving, and the girls bounced.

Chapter 5

Layla woke up to the ring tone of her cell phone and with a slight headache. She looked at the number and pressed ignore. It was already after noon. Layla went to her bathroom, washed her face, and brushed her teeth. Layla started thinking about all the things she would need for her new condo when and if she got it. She went to her safe, which sat in the back of her closet, opened it, and grabbed the money. She counted out sixty one-hundred dollar bills, twenty-three fifty dollar fills, forty-one twenty dollar bills, and didn't bother counting out the tens, fives, and all the one dollar bills she had. She knew she would just bet that money on side bets with the little youngins that wanted in on the game. That gave Layla a total of seven thousand, nine hundred and seventy dollars in big bills.

"This is not going to get it." Layla said out loud while looking at the money. She jumped up, grabbed the phone and dialed Yve.

Yve was just walking in the house from getting breakfast with Jayden. When she got in last night, he was asleep and so she had quietly came in the room and taken off her clothes. As soon as she got in the bed, he woke up. He grabbed her and held her close, which was a nice gesture since she was tired. She had known it was too good to be true and as soon as she started to doze off, she felt him playing with her nipples. She didn't feel like having sex so she turned around, scooted down and filled her mouth with his dick. She knew how to make him cum fast and was determined to do just that so she could get some sleep. With all the sounds she made with her mouth, Yve made Jayden cum in less than ten minutes. She got up and went to the bathroom to brush her teeth and gargle. Jayden was knocked out and already snoring when Yve returned and got back in bed.

After returning from breakfast, Yve turned around and waved goodbye to Jayden who was waiting for her to get all the way in the door. Yve dropped her purse on the kitchen counter and ran upstairs and grabbed her iPod to play while she was downstairs. From upstairs she heard her cell phone ringing and quickly went back downstairs to answer it. She didn't recognize the number but answered it any way.

"Hello?"

"This Levi, is Yve available."

"Hi, Levi. This is me, how you doing?" Yve put the iPod in and turned the volume down low and went and sat on her bear rug that was in the middle of the floor.

"I'm good. Running a few errands and thought I would call to see if I can see your pretty face today. Speaking of which, I saw a picture of you today? Matter of fact, a lot of them."

Yve already knew he was referring to the all-white party flier that she had recently did a photo session for and she figured the fliers must have been circulating heavy since the party was in a few weeks.

"Oh, really. And where did you see that at?"

"At my store. The promoter came by and asked us to sell tickets for his party and being as though I don't turn down money, I told him yeah, we could do that. So, he left the tickets and the fliers. You looking real cute in your little white Angel outfit, Shawty."

"Aww, thanks, Levi. So, what did you have in mind?"

"I was thinking I can come scoop you up and take you to lunch when my brother gets back in here."

"Oh, that will work. I just ate not that long ago so we might – I'm sorry, my other line is beeping, can I put you on hold?" Yve clicked over without waiting for a response.

"Hello?"

"Yve, what you doing?" It was Layla.

"Nothing, talking to Levi on the other line."

"Who is Levi?"

"The dude from the club last night. Duh, Malachi's brother. You know you smoke too much, right?" Yve asked playfully and burst out laughing.

"Whatever. Hater. What he talking about?"

"If you let me get off the phone, I can see. Right now, he just talking about going to lunch."

"Oh, true. I was asking because I wanted you to let me use your car to make a couple of moves. I need to hit a couple of games today and I know niggas is out shooting." Layla said getting hype with just the thought of getting money.

"That's cool. I wasn't doing anything anyway and he was coming to pick me up for lunch. Look, I'm being rude. Get somebody to drop you off."

"Alright. Thanks hun. See you in a few." Layla said, and hung up the phone.

Yve clicked back over and heard Levi talking to some dude in the background asking him what size he was looking for.

"Levi, I'm back. My bad. That was my girl Layla."

"That's the one that Malachi was trying to holler at, right? What's up with shawty? She seemed real stuck up."

"Layla is not stuck up, she is cool but from what I was told, your bother don't know how to approach women. But, anyway, what time are you trying to hook up?" Yve was not about to let him bad mouth Layla so she figured she'd better switch the conversation.

"How about around four since you just got finished eating?"

"Okay, that will work. Call when you need directions."

"Naw, just give me the address and I will put it in the navi."

"The navi? Oh, duh, the navigation system. Okay, it's 610 Naylor Road in Southeast."

"Got it. Are those the townhouses over there?"

"Yeah, I live in the circle at the end of the street."

"Somebody got some money," Levi joked.

"I'd sure like to know who, 'cause it sure ain't me." Yve responded and gave Levi a slight giggle.

"Alright, gorgeous. See you shortly."

"Okay." Yve hung up the phone and decided to just lay there and relax before going to look in her closet to find something sexy to wear. It hadn't been but twenty minutes before she was awakened from the sound of knocks coming at the door.

Damn, I can't get no sleep. Yve went and opened the door without bothering to ask who it was or looking through her peep hole.

"What's up, Hoochie? You must really think you live in the damn country opening doors and what not without asking who the hell it is." Layla mumbled.

"That's 'cause I knew it was your ass." Yve, went back to the living room with Layla hot on her heels.

"No you didn't. Stop lying." Layla sat on the sofa while Yve sat back down on the rug.

"Whatever, I looked through the peep hole."

"Got ya! See, Skank. I told you your ass was lying. I had my finger on the peep hole. See, your ass better act like you know—you live in Southeast, not damn North Carolina with grandma!" Layla was too hyped up for Yve who was tired and wanted to finish taking her nap.

"Damn, I see why Nate ass say you should be a detective. Your ass watch to much damn CSI." Yve said and the girls fell out laughing.

"The keys are on the kitchen table. Please get them and get your ass on so I can take a nap."

Layla got up and went to get the keys from the kitchen. When she returned, she kissed Yve on the cheek. "Thanks, honey. Have a nice lunch and call me when you get back and I will bring you the car."

"Where ya going at to shoot? I might get him to drop me off if I feel like being outside." Yve asked as she got up to walk Layla to the door.

"First back around the way and Al mentioned going uptown around his cousin way."

"Alright, be careful and please don't be letting them niggas sit all up on the hood of the car. I will hit you on your cell."

Yve shut the door behind Layla and headed up the stairs to pick out an outfit for her lunch date. She would still try to catch a quick shut eye before Levi arrived.

Layla jumped in Yve's Silver SC Lexus drop top and put the top back. A Kelly Rowland CD was already in the changer so she decided to let it play. Layla could see how people with short hair could easily love convertibles. She was not feeling it because her hair was blowing all in her face. *Nate better step his game up.* She thought, referring to Yve's car that Demazio had bought her right before they decided to go their separate ways. She couldn't believe that he let her keep it but that was just the kind of person he was.

When Layla pulled up to the park, she could see Al, Sweets and a couple other guys from around the way already heavy in a game. She parked away from where they were so they wouldn't even be tempted to sit on the car and walked over to the game.

"What's up, y'all? I'm about to get in."

"Naw, you are not about to jump in this game. I got too much money out here and I'm trying to get my money back from these niggas." Sweets was always picking with Layla.

"Nigga – you not gonna sit up here and tell me what game I can get in. Who bettin' with his ass, I got two hundred he miss his point."

Everybody knew Sweets had a good shot, so they were all trying to get that bet.

"That's how you going? I got two I make this point." Sweets threw the money beside Layla's feet and she threw hers down.

She also took two other bets from two other guys that took her up on her offer. Sweets rolled the dice and they landed on four.

"Al, what's his point?" Layla asked Al since he was fading Sweets.

"His point is seven," Al laughed sarcastically and stooped down to gate Sweets next roll.

"Here go my point right here. Come on, Nina." Sweets rolled again and they landed on eleven. Al picked up four twenties, which was from their side bet and Sweets threw four more down indicating that he was going back on their bet.

Al gated Sweets next roll, which caused Sweets to get upset. "Nigga you gonna let me roll or you gonna keep doing that girly shit."

"Nigga shut up and roll."

Sweets rolled and the dice landed on seven.

"Damn, that's from all that damn gating and shit. I'm about to run to the house and get some more money. I'll be back."

While Sweets was talking, Layla was collecting her money. Al was counting his money and passed the dice.

Layla picked the dice up. "Let me shoot. Who got me?"

One of the dudes she had just won two hundred from gladly stepped up thinking he was gonna get his money back. The dice had went around plenty of times and Layla got into several of their pockets and was now ready to go since there wasn't much more money out there. It was obvious Sweets wasn't coming back since he had been gone for almost two hours. Al and Layla discussed their next move and decided to go uptown. Layla and Al jumped in Yve's car and were on their way. Layla grabbed her phone and turned the volume back up. She noticed she had two missed calls from Nate and one from an unidentified caller. She called Nate back.

"Hey Nate, what's going on?"

"Where you at? I been calling your phone."

"I was around the way breaking Sweets and them. What's going on?"

"Alright, Baby G. That's what's up. You should've called me and I would've slid through."

"I figured you were probably still sleep from your obvious long night since you didn't call me when you left the club."

"Oh, go 'head with that, I went straight to my mom's house and crashed. I was tore up. But, I'm trying to see you tonight so make it happen."

"Forget you too Trick!" Layla was screaming at a girl who wouldn't let her get over.

"Layla, who the hell you talking to?" Al was cracking up laughing and going through Yve's CD case.

"My bad, Boo. The winch saw me with my blinker on and still wouldn't let me over. But anyway, I'm tired of being your booty call."

"Layla, you need to start acting like a damn lady. Where you on your way to?" Nate totally disregarded Layla's comment because he knew she was much more than that.

"First of all I do act like a lady, but whatever. Me and Al on our way uptown around his cousin way."

"Shawty, Al is cool and all but what I tell you about shooting with every damn body. All niggas ain't for no female taking their money off their street hustle. Please don't make me have to catch a case out this joint cause your stupid ass out there getting niggas money."

"Boo, don't worry. I'm good. I will hit you when I leave."

"Yeah, okay. Tell Al I said to hit me later to talk about that move he was telling me about."

"What move?"

"There you go being nosey. Mind your business and just tell him what I said." Nate hung up and Layla told Al what Nate said. But not before trying to find out what move Nate was referring to.

Al paid Layla no mind and turned up the volume to hear the CD he had just popped in.

Before they arrived at their destination, Layla made a few more calls. She called Monique but she was busy doing some girl hair so she told her she would see her later and then she called the condo leasing office to see what happened with her application. To her surprise, Cookie told her she was all set and could move in her new condo on the first of the month, which was only two weeks away. Layla was ecstatic and couldn't wait to tell the girls. All she could think about is getting money at this game with Al to purchase the things she will need for her new home.

Chapter 6

Levi pulled up to Yve's townhouse and was glad it wasn't what he imagined with a lot of people hanging out in the neighborhood. He got out the car and walked to her door. Just as he was about to ring the doorbell, Yve came out.

"Hey Levi. I see you found me okay." Yve was dressed in a cream sundress with brown sandals and she carried her Louis Vuitton clutch that was only big enough for her necessities.

"Hi beautiful. Yeah, I found you and you are looking more beautiful than last night. You ready?" Levi held out his arm for Yve to hold while she came down the one step. He had on blue jeans, a Hermano blue button down shirt with white writing, fresh white Air Force Ones, and enough bling to outdo the sun.

"Yeah, I'm ready and thank you. You look okay too." Yve smiled and Levi laughed at her comment knowing that he was looking good.

On the ride to the restaurant, Yve set back and enjoyed the plush leather seats in his 750, black on black BMW. She was impressed because not too many brothers his age could afford such a car. Especially, if he afforded it legally, which is what she assumed until she was told or saw differently. Levi pushed in an oldies but goodies CD and turned the volume down low so the two of them could talk.

"Are you comfortable?" Levi turned towards Yve for a response.

"Umm, where is the seat adjuster? Does your car have enough buttons or what?" Yve was busy trying to find the button on the side of her seat.

"Here it is, honey." Levi pointed to the buttons that were shaped like a chair that Yve failed to notice on her left side near the console.

"Oh, okay." Yve felt kind of silly but brushed it off.

"So, where are we headed?"

"I was thinking of heading downtown to Georgia Brown's unless you would like to go somewhere else." Yve was impressed that he already had somewhere in mind.

"No, that's fine. Actually, I've never eaten there before. They have Soul Food, right?"

"Yeah, one of the best in our area." Levi stated and turned the volume up as they cruised downtown.

When they arrived to the restaurant, the valet attendant opened Yve's door and then ran over to try to catch Levi before he opened his door. Levi tipped the attendant a twenty dollar bill and instructed him to be extremely careful with his baby. The attendant thanked him and assured him he would take good care of his beautiful car.

When the two entered the restaurant, Yve was very impressed with the ambience. She couldn't believe how elegant the restaurant was decorated and she loved the fact that the lights were dim and provided a great atmosphere for intimate conversation. The host who seemed to know Levi personally escorted them to a table in the back of the restaurant where it seemed it was reserved just for them. The host pulled out her chair and waited for her to get comfortable before handing them both menus. Yve finally noticed the rose sitting on her plate with a little card attached. She smiled at Levi and thought about how this nigga was pulling out all the stops. She read the card: *Roses are red and things are not always right but I'm hoping my world will change after our encounter tonight.*

"This is so sweet. Thank you."

Even though the riddle kind of through her off, she let it be. She figured Levi was trying to be romantic and rhyme at the same time. She had to admit that he definitely had her attention. Lunch went great. They both took the time to get to know each other. Yve opened up to Levi and explained that she was raised by her grandmother and that her mom passed away when she was young. He asked about her father and she reluctantly explained that she never knew him. Levi could tell that she was getting a little uncomfortable so he switched the conversation.

"You didn't tell me happy birthday," Levi said to Yve and waited for her response.

"What? It's your birthday and you didn't tell me?" Yve didn't believe him so she asked to see his driver's license. Sure enough, it was.

"How could you not tell me? You could have told me earlier. I would have at the least got you a card." Yve smiled.

"Don't worry about it, ma. I got something else in mind you can do for me." Yve looked at Levi liked he had lost his mind. She thought for sure he had her confused with somebody else.

"Excuse me?"

Levi looked at her and quickly tried to rephrase what he had just said. "Naw, it's not like that. My bad. What I meant was that I have something to ask you but I'm not sure how you will react."

"Just ask me. All I can say is yes or no, right."

Levi knew he was reaching but decided to just ask her. "I know the card seemed kind of confusing because I said tonight and it's not even six o'clock yet but I was wondering if you wouldn't mind taking a last minute trip with me." Yve looked at Levi and almost spit out her champagne. "What do you mean a trip? Tonight?"

Yve was ready to call Layla and tell her to come pick her up. She thought for sure this nigga was tripping.

"Look, I know we just met and all but it's a fashion show taking place in Vegas tomorrow and I was debating on whether I wanted to go. They sent tickets for me and my brother and seeing that it's my birthday, I figured we can just go. It can be my present from you."

Yve looked at him and was flattered that he would consider taking her with him but she didn't know enough about him to feel comfortable flying to Vegas with him. She thought about it for a minute and then thought about Layla. Her girl would love to go to Vegas and gamble with the big dawgs.

"I tell you what, I will go but I don't feel right going alone. Can my girls go too?" Levi thought about what she asked and was like why not. It was his birthday so he could afford to splurge.

"Okay, you can bring your girls."

Yve jumped up and gave him a hug and thanked him. "So, if the fashion show is tomorrow, when will we leave?"

"In a very few." He picked up the phone and started making calls.

Yve interrupted him. "Wait a minute. I need to go home and pack and I have to call my girls."

"Y'all don't need to pack anything beautiful. You're with me. We don't take bags with us. Too much hassle. We will go shopping when we get there."

Yve couldn't believe her luck. She was use to nice things and all but this was a whole different ball game for her. Shit, she had never just gone out of town on the whim without clothes and what not. She quickly called Layla and Monique. She hung up and called Layla three times back to back before she answered.

"Yve, you know I must be shooting if I don't answer the phone. You just messed up my shot and had me crap out. Girl, this better be important."

"If you shut the hell up and stop yapping I can tell you that we are going on a trip."

"Hold up. I will fade you. Just give me a minute."

Al noticed the dude was getting a little impatient with Layla so he told him he would fade him until she got off the phone.

"Yeah, I'm back. Girl, niggas be pressed and act like they can't wait a damn minute. So, what are you talking about? We going on a trip to where? I am not trying to go down North Carolina to see grandma this week, Yve. I need to get this paper for my new condo."

"Shit, you got it?" Yve was more excited than Layla. "That's what's up Boo! Naw, we are not going to North Kakilacki. We going to Vegas."

"Stop playing! Layla was about to get hype. For real Chica? When?" Layla had completely stepped off from the game so no one could hear her conversation.

"That's the catch, we're kind of leaving tonight." Yve whispered.

Layla looked at the phone and knew her girlfriend was tripping. "What do you mean tonight? We don't have tickets or anything. Plus, I need to be able to run home and pack."

"No time."

Levi interrupted Yve's conversation with Monique. "Beautiful, we need to be at the airport in less than an hour. Our plane is leaving at eight thirty."

Layla could hear Levi in the background. "Who is that and who is we?"

"Oh, that's Levi and he is the one taking us to Vegas. It's his birthday and there is a fashion show there tomorrow. Look, I don't have time to explain it all right now. Just meet me at Reagan National in half an hour."

Layla was getting more excited by the minute. "Dang, this some real gangsta stuff. What about Monique?"

"If you get off the phone, I can call her." Yve said. "Just keep your phone on and park my car in the daily parking garage. Layla make sure you lock it up real good and call me when you get there."

"Well, at least tell me what airline we're leaving from?" Layla could hear Yve asking Levi in the background.

She came back to the phone. "United Air and it shouldn't take you long since you're uptown."

"Alright. I'm on the way. Thanks dawg for looking out. You know your girl gonna get her man in Vegas on those tables." Yve and Layla both laughed and disconnected the call.

Yve quickly dialed Monique and explained to her the situation and informed her that she needed to meet them at the airport in less than an hour. Monique being the sensible one and the mother hen told her she had lost her mind to up and just roll to Vegas with a dude she had just met. Levi was paying the bill and still making phone calls. It was no convincing Monique at such short notice to stop everything and roll to Vegas with them.

"Just have fun for me because I can't just up and leave. I was on my way out with my new friend Carlos so y'all just be careful and hit me when y'all get there. Oh, and Yve – send me a text with his information."

"Okay, Mother." Yve was not happy with Monique not going but didn't have enough time to convince her to go so she decided to just let it go.

Yve and Levi were already in the car and heading to the airport. He had overheard Yve's conversation and decided to tell his brother just to close the store for a couple of days and meet him at the airport to take Monique's ticket.

Yve was thrilled and couldn't wait to get to Vegas to shop. She was so deep in her own thoughts that she didn't hear him call Malachi. She was too busy thinking of what she was going to get while in Vegas. She also knew if he was giving her any money to play with, she would be pocketing that too since she doesn't gamble. She may play a slot machine here and there but nothing like Layla. She knew girlfriend will be in heaven and can't wait to share this experience with her.

When they arrived at the airport, they started looking for a parking space. Levi was carefully looking for the perfect parking space to leave his baby. He would have never parked his car at the airport if it wasn't such last minute. He would have made sure one of his boys dropped him off and came and got him.

Yve was busy on the phone with Layla trying to get her exact location. They decided to just meet at the ticket counter. Levi had arranged for open tickets and they would have to show their I.D. to get their boarding passes. Levi had finally found a suitable park and they were on their way to the ticket counter to get their boarding passes. Yve spotted Layla first.

"What's up, Chica?" Yve yelled and ran over to give Layla a hug.

"What's up, Mamasita." Layla responded.

Yve held Layla back and took a look at her. "When did you have time to change?"

Layla spun around showing off her cute light pink BEBE sweat suit that hugged all her curves with the tennis shoes to match.

"Girl, you know I am always prepared. I had to have something in my bag just in case it got cool while I was out on the block. Where is Monique?"

"Girl, Monique said she can't just up and roll like that. You know how motherly she can be. She told us to have fun and hit her when we get back." Yve said and moved out of Layla's way so she could speak to Levi.

"Hi Levi. Thanks for the trip and definitely good looking out."

"It ain't nothing baby girl. I'm sure I will get this change and a lot more betting with you once we hit the tables," Levi joked.

They were next in line so they all took out their licenses and went to the ticket counter.

The lady took all their licenses and asked whether they had luggage that needed to be checked in. They each answered no. She asked for the credit card that Levi had used to make the reservation. He gave her his Visa Black Card and mentioned that there may or may not be another passenger depending on if he made it on time. She asked for the name and when he said Malachi, the look on both Yve and Layla's face was priceless.

"Yve what the hell is going on?" Layla tried whispering but Levi overheard her.

"Shawty, it definitely is not what you think. The two of you will have your own room and so will me and my brother. Your girl was supposed to go but because she didn't, I told my brother to come roll. I didn't want to waste my money since the ticket was non-refundable."

Layla was not hearing it and just knew this was a set up. She didn't give a damn one way or the other. She will just ignore Malachi the entire time.

"But, from the looks of it, he won't make it here in time anyway. Relax Layla. My brother is definitely a good dude. That's my word." Levi nudged Layla's arm and smiled, which helped ease the tension that was building in the air.

Because they were flying first class, they didn't have to wait in the long security line that would have surely caused them to miss their flight. By the time they went through security and were seated at the gate, it was fifteen minutes to boarding. Levi tried calling Malachi several times but kept getting his voicemail. Layla and Yve were in the Newsstand Store buying magazines and candy for their seven hour flight.

When the girls returned, it was time for the first class passengers to board. It took about twenty minutes For the entire flight to be seated.

"See, Shawty, I told you not to get all bent out of shape. Malachi didn't even make it." Levi said to Layla and ordered a bottle of Chardonnay for the three of them to sip on. The flight attendant was calling final boarding to all passengers. Just as she was making the announcement, Malachi walked on. He sat in an empty seat, which was in the row behind Layla and Yve. Levi noticed him and gave him a head nod because Malachi had his finger up to his lips indicating that he didn't want them to know he had made it. The stewardess brought them a bottle of champagne and three glasses. Layla was the first to speak as the stewardess opened the champagne and filled all three glasses.

"To a fun, exciting, money making trip and happy birthday Levi," Layla said and raised her glass.

Levi and Yve toasted with her and agreed by clinking their glasses along with hers. Malachi had already managed to get a glass from one of the other stewardess and reached over the seat to toast with them.

"I'll toast to that. Hit me, bro." Malachi winked at Layla as Levi poured champagne in his glass.

Layla was at a loss for words. She said the only thing she could manage to say. "Damn."

Chapter 7

Layla and Yve slept most of the plane ride while Malachi and Levi were mostly talking business and getting nice off the three bottles of champagne they ordered. The plane landing was so shaky that it woke both Layla and Yve.

"Ladies and Gentlemen, thank you for flying United Air. We have safely arrived in Las Vegas and the time is now 12:30am. The weather here is clear and the temperature is eighty-five degrees. We thank you again and wish you good luck here in Sin City." The passengers began applauding and whistling. Layla and Yve both were stretching and a little irritable. Layla searched through her bag for gum and quickly popped it in her mouth and gave Yve a piece and they all hurriedly exited the plane.

The first stop was the restroom for the girls. Layla washed her face and brushed her teeth. She gave Yve the extra toothbrush she had in her bag so she could do the same.

"Okay, we need to hurry up and get me some tennis shoes or something. I have got to take these sandals off." Yve said while she slipped her sandals off and brushed her teeth.

"Yeah, I know you are ready to take them shoes off. We won't be able to go shopping until the morning." Layla said.

"Girl, we are in the city that never sleeps. I know I should be able to find some flip flops at the least. Layla, I know you are going to be nice, right? They didn't have to invite us so just be cordial." Yve was looking at Layla through the mirror while freshening up her make-up.

"Yes, girl. It's all good. Malachi is cool and sexy as hell. He just needs to come correct, that's all. He will figure it out."

As they exited the restroom, the guys were waiting patiently for them. "Y'all looking good." Malachi said as he made his way over to walk beside Layla.

"We need to find somewhere to get Yve some tennis shoes or flip flops from... Damn, they got slot machines in the airport?" Layla was loud enough for everyone around her to hear. "They not playing. They want all your change soon as you land in this mother."

Levi, Yve, and Malachi were laughing at Layla.

"Yes, they do so remember that when you playing in the casino. You can't break them. Their money is much longer than yours," Malachi said.

"Yeah, true that." Layla said and kept walking.

When they got in the cab the girls were fully awake and excited. Yve commented about how glitzy and glamorous everything was. It reminded her of all the many movies she had seen that took place in Vegas. Her favorite being Casino with Al Pacino.

"Look at the beautiful waterfall and the lights." Layla was mesmerized by the hotel water show.

"Bellagio Hotel," the cab driver announced and got out to open the passenger door.

Malachi gave him the fare and a tip and they all walked into the hotel. While the guys were checking in, Malachi noticed a shop that was open and looked as if it sold everything under the sun.

"Yve, go check out that spot over there and see if they have some shoes you can slip on." Malachi reached in his pocket and gave Yve and Layla a hundred dollars. "Grab whatever other little items y'all might need."

After checking in, dropping off the things the girls just purchased, and admiring the rooms they were right back out and headed to the casino. While on the elevator ride down, Layla had mentioned that she was approved to move in her condo in just a few weeks. She was understandably happy and it showed all in her face. Layla's phone rang and she looked at the caller ID. It was Nate. She pressed the ignore button because she didn't want to be rude. She made a mental note to call him back when she was alone. This was the first time she had actually thought about him since first getting the call from Yve. She felt she needed this time away from him. She wanted him to miss her and thought that maybe that will eventually make him want her like she wanted him.

When they walked into the casino, Layla felt a serious rush. She felt like this was where she needed to be. Yve and Levi walked off and told them they would meet at the bar in an hour or so to grab something to eat.

Malachi escorted Layla to a crap table that wasn't that crowded. Layla looked at the table and was a bit confused because there were so many different sections on the table that she was unfamiliar with. Malachi took out a wad of money wrapped up in a rubber band and counted out twenty one hundred dollar bills and threw them on the table. Layla took out ten bills and did the same. Malachi was tickled that Layla was so down and still maintained an innocence about her that made him want to just protect her. Malachi was going to give her a thousand of the money he just put down but didn't say anything because he didn't want to offend her after she had took out her money. Malachi bet on the pass line and instructed Layla to do the same. Since they gave them only hundred dollar chips, Layla figured that was the minimum bet at the table and that was why it wasn't a lot of people like the other tables that was full of people. Malachi started explaining to Layla what all of the different betting options were and what bets were considered good and foolish bets. He stressed to Layla how the field bet wasn't a good move but Layla liked the field because she felt it was in her favor with so many numbers. There was only three other people at the table and while Malachi was betting just about every option on the table, Layla decided to lay low and wait for her turn to roll. It was finally her turn and on her first roll she hit eleven, she won everyone at the table money and rolled again. Layla had a good feeling so she put five hundred dollars on the field. She rolled a four and was so elated.

"That's what's up!" Malachi couldn't believe she put so much on the field but figured since it worked for her he would let her do her thing. The cocktail waitress came around and Layla ordered a double shot of Ciroc on the rocks.

Malachi ordered a double shot of patron and gave the waitress a hundred dollar bill and asked her to keep them coming. He knew how long they normally took to come around because the alcohol was free. If they knew what he knew, they would come around more often because alcohol get you loose and make you start spending that dough faster. Layla was killing the table betting on the field. She only lost a couple of times and thankfully it was only when she lowered her bet. She finally crapped out but it was definitely a good roll. She had won over three thousand dollars by backing up her original bet on the pass line like Malachi instructed and by betting five hundred and sometimes eight hundred on the field. When she did lose on the field she only had two hundred on it so it didn't really have an impact on her stack.

"Malachi, what's the numbers right there in the center for? The four, six, eight, and ten?" Layla was pointing at the bets that were considered the hard bets.

"If you bet on them and they land the way they are showing on the board, then you get seven to ten times your bet."

"That's the hard ways. I got a hundred on each of those. Those are really good bets because you win so much but they can only come that way," Malachi told Layla while pointing at the board. "If they come any other way, you lose and they will more than likely ask you if you want to go back."

"Oh, okay. Sort of like betting the back of the dice like six-eight or five-nine?" Layla was definitely soaking in the game and trying to learn as much as possible. She was in the zone.

Malachi chuckled. "Not really but you on the right track."

Malachi admired the way Layla ass jiggled every time she got excited and jumped up and down. He was feeling nice and his drink was definitely settling in. His stomach started growling. He looked at his watch and told Layla it was time to go meet Levi and Yve. Layla reluctantly grabbed her chips and was about to walk off before Malachi instructed her to put them on the table so the dealers and host could cash her out. Layla was given four orange chips, a purple chip, some black and some green. She had a total of four thousand, eight hundred and seventy five dollars. To say the least, Layla was thrilled. Malachi had a total of seven thousand, nine hundred and some change. They went to the cashier to get the cash and Layla stuffed hers in her pink Chanel bag that matched her sweat suit. When Malachi received his cash, he peeled off the two thousand he had started with and put it back on his wad of money and gave Layla the Five thousand

and change and told her to get something nice for her condo that he hoped he would have the privilege of seeing once they returned. Layla was shocked at his generosity and that alone made her moist.

"Thank you, Malachi. I will do just that." Layla took the money and put it in her bag as they headed to the bar to meet Levi and Yve.

The girls hugged each other which indicated they were equally excited by their surroundings and the guys gave dap and they all went and sat at the bar.

"Layla, how did you do on the table?" Levi asked her already knowing if nothing else she did good since he know she wasn't spending her own money given the type of dude his brother was.

Layla couldn't hold back the huge grin on her face. "I did good. I walked away a couple thousand richer."

"Damn, Layla. That's what's up." Yve said as she gave her girl a high five.

The bartender came over and they each ordered drinks and something to snack on to hold them until the morning.

"So, what's good? What time we have to get up in the morning, yo?" Malachi asked Levi.

"The fashion show starts at like four so y'all be ready to get up around ten so we can go shopping and get something to eat before the show." Levi instructed and took a swig of his drink and then continued. "We got a meeting right after the show so that will give you ladies a chance to play some more or shop and then we're heading home on a red eye flight."

Malachi and Levi started discussing business. Yve and Layla excused themselves and went to the bathroom. Soon as they left the table the girls started talking.

"Girl, you not gonna believe Malachi gave me his winnings from the table, which was a little over five thousand dollars and told me to get something for the condo. Now, that's gangsta right there." Layla giggled while coming out the stall and washing her hands.

Yve was equally excited and told Layla that Levi had gave her two thousand just to play the damn slots.

"Girl, and you know damn well most of that is in my damn pocket. I wish the hell I would give all that money to the damn casino." Yve said while looking in the mirror and running her hands through her hair trying to spike it back up. "Girl, Levi is sexy as hell and not stingy by far." I know I shouldn't but I am feeling nice as off the drinks and my pussy is getting wetter by the damn minute. I am going to tap that ass." Yve burst out laughing at her own self. Both girls were definitely drunk.

"You can do whatever you want. You a grown ass woman but just make sure you use protection Chica." Layla said while refreshing her lips with liner and gloss. "All I know is that Malachi better not try anything. So, how the hell are you going to tell him that you want to stay in the room with him and send Malachi over to ours?" Layla questioned.

"Girl, you know damn well I don't have no cut cards. I'm just going to tell him that your ass want to be alone with Malachi." Yve said and started wobbling out the door.

"Oh, no your ass ain't. No cut cards my ass." Layla said while laughing and walking behind Yve back to the bar where the guys were.

The wings, chicken fingers, fries, and steam shrimp they all ordered were there and the guys were already feasting.

"Y'all couldn't wait for us before y'all got started?" Yve said as they sat back down. She ordered her and Layla another drink and licked her lips at Levi seductively.

"I don't need another drink. I am already feeling it some kind of terrible." Layla said and started eating.

"Girl, your ass is in Vegas, so drink the hell up." Yve slurred and they all start laughing.

They finally finished eating and it was now three o'clock in the morning. The guys suggested going back to the room so they can be ready to get up in a couple of hours to start shopping. That was enough to get the girls moving. Yve had already whispered to Levi that she wanted to stay in the room with him and that Layla wouldn't mind Malachi staying in their room with her. So, Levi had put Malachi on point so by the time they got upstairs, no words were needed to discuss the change of plans. It's not like they had luggage and so forth so Yve just went to get her toothbrush, soap, and other toiletries she had purchased while in the lobby and went to what was supposed to be Levi and Malachi's room and shut the door behind her.

Malachi and Layla were both drunk and tired. Layla took her clothes off and went to take a shower. When she came back in the room, Malachi was under the covers with only his boxers on and snoring. Layla said a silent prayer of thanks for the day's events, asked God to watch over her family, friends, and Nate and got in the bed and immediately fell asleep.

In the room next door, Yve was utilizing all the hotels amenities, which included a glass of champagne from the mini bar and a nice bubble bath in the Jacuzzi. Levi was on his cell phone speaking to someone who was obviously there in Vegas because he was telling them that he was in the room and would see them first thing in the morning. Yve was feeling really nice and prayed that she wouldn't have a hangover in the morning. She got out the tub and dried herself off. She walked back in the room just as Levi was coming in the bathroom. *Damn, he looks good. Nice body, money, good conversation. This brother got it going on and seems to be legit. He is definitely my kind of nigga,* Yve was thinking while not realizing that she was licking her lips.

"You see something you like?" Levi said and brought her back to the moment.

"Oh, hell yeah. I sure do, Birthday Boy." Yve said as she started kissing him.

"Good, beautiful. Hold that thought while I jump in the shower and try not to fall asleep." Levi smacked her ass and continued in the bathroom.

Yve wasn't thinking about sleeping because she was throbbing and she needed a fix. She put Victoria Secret Pear lotion that she got from Layla all over her body and sat in the middle of the bed and started playing with herself. When she was almost at her climax, she heard the shower turn off. She calmed herself down not to cum and put two of her fingers in her pussy. Levi opened the door and was drying off. His body was looking so good she didn't even stop. She continued to play with herself as he stood there watching her and stroking his dick. No words were needed for the nightcap that was about to take place. Levi cut the light off and walked to the bed.

"Wait, let me." Levi said as he lay in between her legs and rocked her world.

BABY G

Chapter 8

Meanwhile, on the East Coast, Nate and Al were crashed at Nate's apartment from being up all night discussing their plans to catch these stick up dudes that had caught Nate slipping a year ago. Nate had a heart and didn't want to kill them but definitely wanted to send a message. They really didn't get nothing from him but a grand and a little work he had on him. The night they caught him he was on his way home from the club and was so twisted that he ended up falling asleep in the parking lot. Apparently they saw him in the car, put a plan together where he didn't even have time to grab his Glock, and the rest is history. Nate never knew who the youngins were because they all wore masks but Al's cousin, Lashone, messed with one of them from time to time and they got careless and started reminiscing while drunk one night. Lashone had known about Nate's incident and didn't hesitate to call her favorite cousin to tell him what she had heard knowing that Al and Nate were close. She explained to Al that they were all chilling at her place and were drinking and planning this other job when they started joking around stating how they wish it could be as easy as the joint they pulled off in Greenbelt when the drunken clown fell asleep in the car. She further informed him that they were planning another move within the next couple of days in which they were going to break into the cats store from New York that was supposedly just a front for a drug operation they were running. From eavesdropping, she was able to find out that one of the girls that worked in the store tipped her brother off about the safe that was in the office and the traffic that she had witnessed coming in and out of the store. The sister also told him that she could tell that the dudes that were coming in and out of the store were workers that reported directly to the two owners. Anybody that was anybody knew that *Hermanos* was just a front and that's how most people kept the feds out of their hair and able to clean their illegal money. Reason being was because the so called brothers came up to DC and was able to open up the store and was hot off the break. Not known to happen in the city because DC residents are known to be extremely anal about their style and most importantly, their clothes. The district might have been the last to get a lot of things but they were certainly on top of the fashion game. Number one reason being is that most niggas that had the money traveled for their gear and it was serious to be called a bamma, which meant just the opposite of the true meaning in DC. Not to mention that for the store to be in DC, you didn't see heaps of people rocking the label. However, the owners always represented their label well.

Nate and Al's plan was flawless. They had planned to follow the youngins once they left and made sure they would be able to put a trail on them by having Lashone call the dude over her house the day of the job. Niggas never turn down sex. So when he left, they were following him and eventually them. Nate, like everything else, was able to get some heavy machinery even though they didn't think they would need it but made sure to have it on hand. He copped several police issued nine millimeters and a gage. Nate wasn't a killer but definitely would do what he had to do if it became a choice of him or them.

Malachi was the first to wake up. He got up, took a shower and put his same clothes back on. He pulled the drapes back in the hotel to let the sun wake Layla up. He was standing in front of the bed admiring her sleeping. She had just enough thigh hanging from under the covers to make him rise. She tossed and turned and threw the pillow on her head.

"Can you please close the damn curtains?" Layla was obviously irritated and cranky and it didn't faze Malachi any. He laughed and shook his head.

"Time to get up. We got a lot to do in just a couple of hours so go to the bathroom and freshen up so we can get up out of here." Malachi said while picking up the phone and calling his brother's room.

Yve picked it up after three rings since she was closest to the phone.

"Yeah?" she sounded horrible.

"Damn, don't you think you might want to go brush your teeth before you kill my brother." Malachi said while laughing. Layla rolled her eyes at him and went to the bathroom.

"Shut up Malachi. What time is it?" Yve sat up to look at the clock. She must have moved to fast because she suddenly felt a sharp pain in her head to let her know she had a hangover.

"Shit." Yve said out loud while grabbing her head.

"What's wrong?" Malachi asked sounding real concerned.

"Nothing, I just got a slight hangover. Levi, wake up." Yve tapped Levi a couple of times and turned back towards the phone. "Alright, we getting up. Give us twenty minutes and we will be ready." Yve said and hung up the phone without waiting for a response.

When Malachi hung up the phone, Layla opened the bathroom door. "Malachi, can you hand me my backpack?"

Malachi looked around the room and saw her Gucci backpack sitting on the floor leaning on a chair.

"This bag heavy, what the hell you got up in there?" Malachi asked while handing Layla the bag.

"Just stuff I need." Layla said as she took the bag, gave Malachi a smile, and turned back around towards the sink.

After about thirty minutes they were ready and heading down to the lobby. The guys went and paid for another night stay so they would have somewhere to leave their shopping bags when they returned.

The first stop was the Starbucks in the lobby. Layla and Yve both got hot sweet drinks and doughnuts while the guys got breakfast sandwiches and orange juice to drink. The second stop was Caesar's Palace. Layla and Yve felt like they were in heaven with all the expensive shops that surrounded them. Not to mention, they didn't have to spend a dime of their money. Malachi and Levi definitely knew how to spoil a woman and they received the royal treatment. After easily spending a little over ten grand on both ladies on items such as hand bags, clothes, and shoes; Malachi and Levi took them over to the Venetian Hotel, which was fairly renovated with plenty of new high end stores that included the Cartier Shop. They surprised the girls and brought them both Cartier watches. It took some convincing but the guys both put up half and purchased Monique one as well to stop Yve and Layla from whining about how their girl was going to feel so left out. Layla and Yve heads were gassed up and both couldn't wait to put on one of their new outfits for the fashion show. Even though the show started at 4pm, they knew they needed to be fly as hell. The girls wanted to be sexy and look damn good on Levi and Malachi's arms since they didn't hesitate to pull out all the stops for them.

Time was winding down and the girls were exhausted. They grabbed lunch at the Morton's Steak house in the Mandalay Bay hotel and got stuffed. It was two o'clock and the girls were tired. The guys told them they could take an hour or two to nap and meet them at the Convention Center if they wanted. Layla and Yve happily accepted

the offer. They all went back to the hotel. The guys got dressed and said they were going to take care of some business and would meet them at the Convention Center no later than four thirty. Layla and Yve both went in their rooms.

"Call and get us a wakeup call for three forty-five," Layla said to Yve while unlocking her door.

"Alright, which outfit are you wearing?" Yve asked Layla.

"I think I will wear one of the dresses with sandals."

"Cool, that's a bet." Yve said and they both went in their rooms with nothing but rest on their minds. Little did either of them know that the guys were on their way to meet their connect.

Layla looked at her new watch to see what time it was and called Nate.

"Oh, you can finally return a nigga call." Nate answered on the first ring.

"Hey babe, what's up?" Layla was happy to hear his voice.

"Ain't shit up. You couldn't tell that nigga to let you breathe for a minute." Nate said with heavy sarcasm in his voice.

"Nate, please. Don't start because it's not even like that. Yve and I had a move to make but will be back home early in the morning."

"Oh, yeah? So, what niggas are y'all with?" Nate was upset but knew he really couldn't be so he joked it off.

"Can you tell that nigga to buy me something too?" He knew how to piss Layla off because she was on the other end steaming.

"Nate, I see you got jokes so I will see you tomorrow." Layla hung up the phone before Nate could respond. He didn't bother to call her back because he too was mad. He wasn't certain she was with a nigga but it wasn't like her to not keep in touch so he assumed the worse.

Two hours later, the girls were walking out of the hotel and into a cab. Layla and Yve looked stunning. Layla had on a strapless black baby doll dress that she picked up from a boutique and black pumps that showed off her sexy legs while Yve wore a fitting mermaid style dress that hugged her curves in all the right places. Being as though Yve was light skin, the aqua color dress and the multi-color pumps she wore brought out her tone. The ladies were sure to stop every man in their tracks.

When they arrived at the Convention Center, every eye was on them. Yve called Levi to see where they were. Levi told her that they were finishing up a meeting regarding the clothing line and informed her that their tickets were left at will call under Yve's name. The girls got their tickets and went to find their seats, which were in the second row. They couldn't believe they were sitting right behind Jay Z, Beyoncé, Solange and Wale. To say the least, they felt like a million bucks. The fashion show had started and every designer you could think of was featured. The guys arrived about thirty minutes later. Both Layla and Yve were shocked to see them nudge Jay Z and him stand up to give them both hugs followed by Wale. They both gave Beyoncé and Solange pecks on their cheeks and introduced Layla and Yve. The girls spoke and handled the situation with ease. Malachi gave Layla a kiss on the cheek and told her she looked gorgeous while Levi was a little less subtle and kissed Yve long and hard and complimented her on her choice of outfits. A cocktail waitress came by to take their drink orders. Levi ordered a bottle of the famous Krug, Clos du Mesnil and four glasses. The ladies were definitely impressed as they knew the cost of the champagne was an easy seven hundred and probably more considering the event they were at. To say the least, the ladies were loving every minute of being wined by the handsome brothers. Malachi and Layla were noticeably flirting the entire show and couldn't stop giggling. It was obvious that Nate was not on Layla's mind at that moment.

Chapter 9

That Sunday morning when the girls arrived back to DC, they were exhausted. They both promised to call the guys later that day and Yve dropped Layla off at her moms. Layla's mom didn't give her a chance to walk in the door good before she started.

"Layla, where have you been? I've been worried sick." Layla's mom was dressed for church and looked as if she was a minute from walking out the door.

"Hello to you too Ma. I was out with the girls." Layla tried her best to throw the duffel bag that the guys had to purchase each of them in order to get their new articles back home safely down the basement without her mom noticing it.

"Out with the girls, my butt. You can at least have the decency to pick up the phone and call me. And I know you saw me calling you." Layla's mom was not trying to hear Layla's excuses.

"Are you going to church or are you too grown for that too?" Layla's mom was laying it on thick. Layla's dad was walking down the stairs. Layla reached out and gave him a hug and kiss while pouting.

"Mommy, dang – I just walked in the door. Daddy, please tell Mommy to lay off." Layla was willing her father to step in on her behalf.

"I will do no such thing. You need to go get dressed and join us for service. You do all you want during the week and need to give the Lord some of your time too." Layla's dad was now preaching and Layla had heard enough.

"Dang, I can't believe y'all drilling me and I just walked in the door. That's just why I got my own place. Give me twenty minutes to get dressed so I can tell you both about my new condo on the way to church." Layla ran downstairs to take a quick shower and dressed so she could accompany her mom and dad to church.

When they arrived at church, it was crowded as usual but they managed to get a seat in the center with a good view of the pulpit. Layla was extremely tired but managed to sit through the entire service without nodding off. She vowed she was going home to take a nap before doing anything else that day.

Monique was just finishing someone's hair when she picked up the phone to call Layla. The phone went directly to voicemail. She had talked to them earlier when they landed and they had made plans to meet over Monique's house that evening to possibly go out. She hung up and rang Yve's phone. She answered just in time before her machine picked up.

"Yeah." Yve was obviously sleep and didn't like the idea of being awaken.

"What's up, Chica? Y'all need to get the hell up because we are going out tonight. I will be over there in about two hours once I get myself together." Monique held her hand over the phone to tell the girl, she didn't have change. The girl told her not to worry about it and consider it her tip. She took the two bills and set it on the table and walked behind the girl to let her out.

"Who are you talking to?" Yve asked.

"One of my clients nosey. I'm about to take a shower, put my clothes on and be over there. Where is Layla because her phone is off?" Monique was waving goodbye to her client and locked the door.

"Knowing Layla, she is asleep. Call the house phone and see if she answers. You know her moms is in there. Shoot, we should have been going over there for Sunday dinner. You know her moms threw down?" Yve said, thinking about the dinner that Layla's mom probably prepared.

"You ain't never lied. I'm about to call Mrs. Thompson to see if we can come over there. Just make sure you pack your clothes so we can get dressed from over Layla's house." Monique said before getting off the phone with Yve.

"Alright, bet." Yve said and hung up.

When Yve and Monique arrived over Layla's house, it was around seven o'clock and they never did get in contact with Layla earlier. But Mrs. Thompson had told them that she had been in the bed since they returned from church and had only come out of the room to eat and went right back to bed.

"Hi Mrs. Thompson," the girls sang in unison when Layla's mom opened the door.

"Hi Monique and Yve." She opened the door wider and hugged both girls.

"Monique, how is your mom doing?" Layla's mom asked while giving her a hug.

"She is fine, Mrs. Thompson. I went to see her yesterday and took her something to eat. She has a nerve to be trying to gain weight." Monique said giggling.

"You send her my love honey and tell her I am keeping her in my prayers," Mrs. Thompson said and closed the door. "You girls plates are in the oven and that child of mine is downstairs still sleeping I guess. She better not be pregnant either cause who sleeps all day long," said Mrs. Thompson as she retreated up the stairs.

"Pregnant?" Monique and Yve both said at the same time and looked at one another and hurried down the basement.

Layla's door was closed but Yve just opened it without knocking only to find Layla under the covers and knocked out.

"Damn Hoochie, wake up!" Yve shouted and turned the lights on.

"Damn Layla, are you pregnant," Monique said as she sat on the end of Layla's bed.

Layla's room was a nice size with light green paint on the walls and a painting of a forest courtesy of Monique at Layla's request. It was actually really different and painted very well. Yve and Layla always made comments about how Monique should have went to art school or a fashion institute or something because she was so talented but for whatever reason, Monique never pursued it. Layla had dark oak bedroom furniture with a flat screen on the bare wall that didn't have the art and she had several dice scattered all over her dresser. Layla's bed was facing a huge walk in closet that housed all of her many clothes and shoes.

Layla turned over and was noticeably upset. "Why the hell y'all didn't call me, and hell no I am not pregnant."

"Then why are you so cranky and been in the bed all day?" Yve said and grabbed Layla's furry lounge chair from the corner and sat in it.

"Damn, maybe because my ass just got home from a long ass flight and then was dragged to church by my parents and – why the hell am I explaining myself to y'all? Watch out." Layla threw the covers off of her and got out of bed. "I need to go brush my teeth and take a quick shower."

"Well, why you are in the shower, we are going to warm up our plates. We still going out, right?" Monique said as she and Yve walked behind Layla but detoured up the stairs.

"Yeah, we can still go out." Layla mumbled and closed the bathroom door behind her.

Nate and Al were riding downtown to grab something to eat and to finish discussing their plan because if Lashone was right, the youngins were set to make their move the next night. Nate and Al had made sure to purchase black ski mask, fresh Nike boots, and black jump suits earlier that day from stores that sold plenty of the items on a regular basis. Once they disposed of the gear, they definitely didn't want any forensic specialist to be able to pin anything on them just in case the situation got out of hand and messy.

"Are we straight on everything? Did you speak back to Lashone?" Nate was trying to make sure that they left no room for mistakes.

"Yeah, we good. She said that she would call him tomorrow morning to ask him to come break her off. I told her she had to make sure that he was not over her house tonight to ensure that he would want to come in the morning." Al spoke while flipping through the changer to find something else to listen to.

Nate pulled out his cell phone and called Nut to see whether he got rid of the last couple pounds of weed he had left.

"Nut, we riding downtown, are you close by?" Nate could hear some people in the background but mostly he heard a female complaining about Nut answering the phone.

"Yeah, I'm actually down here eating at Clyde's with a friend. The game on so we chilling at the bar. Why don't you slide by to grab that?"

"That's a bet." Nate said and hung up.

Nate made a U-turn in the middle of the street because he had just passed Clyde's a couple of streets back.

Nate and Al were able to find a parking space not far from the restaurant. Soon as they walked in they spotted Nut and a young lady that when she turned around they were able to distinguish it was Lyn.

The guys gave dap and Nate and Al gave Lyn a hug and Nut a look that said, when did this happen. Nut shrugged his shoulders and Nate and Al sat down and ordered a drink to finish watching the Wizards beat up on their opponents.

Nut excused himself and went to his car to grab the wad of money he owed Nate. When he returned Lyn was telling them about a hot party on the waterfront that was taking place that night. They all agreed to meet at the party that night after changing clothes.

Nate and Al walked back towards his truck and Nate dialed Layla's house phone.

"Hello."

"Yeah, this Nate, who this, Yve?" Nate asked.

"Yeah, What's up Nate? Layla is in the shower. What are you up to? Yve asked while flipping through channels on Layla's TV.

"Ain't shit. Y'all going out tonight?"

"As a matter of fact we are. We are all about to get dressed now. Why, where are y'all going?" Monique was in the background telling Yve to tell Nate she said what's up. "Monique said what's up too."

"Tell her I said nothing but money." Nate said while laughing. "We gonna hit that party down H2O on the waterfront. It's supposed to be hot. So, y'all get dressed and meet us down there so we can do it big."

"That's what's up!" Yve shouted and jumped up off the bed and started dancing in place as she hung up the phone.

"What's up? What's popping tonight? Why you all jumping up dancing and what not?" Monique asked Yve and turned on Layla's iPod. Layla walked in and sat on the bed and started putting lotion on her body.

"Your boy just called and said it's a hot party tonight at H2O on the waterfront tonight so we need to make sure we look fierce. I brought two outfits just in case we weren't really doing too much tonight cause you know how you get and will ditch a party fast as a mug to go to somebody's craps party to shoot and shit."

"I'm down, but we don't know how to do anything else but look fierce hoochie." Layla said and got up and started going through her closet. Layla pulled out a metallic baby doll ruffle top that she purchased from *Nordstrom* and some *Citizen* skinny jeans.

"Why are you wearing jeans?" Monique asked Layla.

"Because I really don't feel like wearing a dress or a skirt. Don't worry with my heels and my accessories, I will look good. Trust." Layla said and smiled.

The girls started putting on their clothes. Monique wore a cute grey wrap dress that showed off her long legs with black accessories and black four inch heels. She wore her full thick hair in big curls, which hung down her back. She already knew within two hours her hair would be in a ponytail. Yve wore a purple baby doll V-neck sheer blouse that stopped at her thighs with black leggings and some purple leather python pumps that she purchased while they were in Vegas. To say the least, the girls were surely going to stop traffic tonight. Monique and Yve both put their *Cartier* watches on at the same time to make sure that Monique was watching.

"Damn, what the hell. I know damn well those are not *Cartier* watches? Y'all two are the absolute worse." Monique said while checking out her girls new watches. "Damn, they fly as hell. See, now I really wish I would've went with y'all."

"See, I told your mother hen ass to live a little and roll with us." Yve said.

"Whatever, y'all make me sick." Monique said and pretended to pout. "Naw, it's all good. Y'all have got to meet Carlos though. He was a good reason to stay behind. But damn, I'm not sure good enough to have missed out on such a lavish gift. Y'all wrist are blinding my ass. All I can say is that's hot."

"We thought so too, so that's why the hell we had to whine and beg to make sure your ass got one too." Layla said while pulling out Monique's watch from her backpack.

Monique screamed and jumped up and down and was too excited to stop and put the watch on.

"Damn, stop all that screaming and put the damn watch on." Yve said.

"Right, you know you about to have my moms and dads coming down those stairs in a minute with your crazy ass."

"Aww, thank you both so much. It is so hot. How the hell did you get one of them to buy me a damn watch?" Monique was visibly grateful.

"You welcome, Chica. We will tell you all about the trip on the way to the club. Let's roll." Yve said and grabbed her purse and keys from Layla's bed.

Yve decided to drive her car and Layla and Monique argued over who would squeeze in the little back seat. Layla ended up getting her way and Monique squeezed in the back.

Chapter 10

The girls pulled up to valet and got out the car. Layla had just got off the phone with Nate and knew he was only about five minutes away. Yve gave the attendant a twenty for the parking and a five dollar tip. He thanked her and pulled off in her baby testing the power.

"Oh, no his ass ain't driving my damn car like that." Yve said, while looking at another attendant. He shrugged his shoulders and walked to the next car behind them hoping she would walk away.

"Girl, come on and stop tripping." Monique said while grabbing Yve's arm.

"Nate and them are in the valet line now. Do y'all want to wait for them or go ahead in?" Layla asked and popped a piece of chewing gum in her mouth. Both Monique and Yve had their hands out indicating they wanted a piece too.

They decided to wait for them to get to the front. Al was the first to jump out while Nate was handing over his keys and paying the attendant.

"Hey ladies," Al said while walking up the ramp to the club. They each exchanged hugs while Nate took his time strolling up.

Nate walked up and grabbed Layla and gave her a hug and a kiss on the mouth, which was not like him but she figured he must've really missed her. She hugged him back and he spoke to Monique and Yve and gave them both hugs.

"Where is Delonté?" Monique asked Nate.

"He's supposed to be meeting us up here. Why you want to know where he is. My man said you ain't giving up no ass." Nate joked. Monique playfully punched Nate in his arm and rolled her eyes.

"Whatever, nigga. He ain't ready, that's why." Monique shot back and they all laughed and walked towards the door. Al paid for Monique and Yve to get in and since Layla was in front of Nate, she thought she would surprise him and pay their way in the club.

They charged her fifty for not having to wait in line and for the charge to enter the club and seventy for Nate. "Damn, ma. That's what's up. Can you get him to give me some dollars too?" Nate sarcastically said and walked in front of Layla.

"What the hell are you tripping off of? Since when I need a nigga to do shit for me?" Layla asked and her and the girls excused themselves to the restroom. The club was jumping and the girls were getting stopped by just about every nigga before finally making it to the ladies room.

"Damn, they act like they have never seen a damn woman before." Monique said while fixing her hair in the mirror.

"Don't blame them, they just haven't seen any as fine as us." Layla said. "I can't believe Nate is starting already. The nigga don't want to be in a relationship but he always got some smart shit to say out of his mouth."

"Girl, you know that is his way of showing you that he care. Stop tripping and let's enjoy tonight. Just think, you move next week and your ass won't be able to go anywhere once them bills kick in." Yve said and laughed.

"You right about that. Y'all ready?" Monique asked.

The girls followed behind her directly to the bar. They purchased a bottle of Moët and got three glasses and went to a nearby sofa. The club was extremely top notch with marble floors and oak stained walls throughout with three different dance floors. The VIP was in the back and was not where the party was at. As far as the girls were concerned, they wanted to be seen and the only way to do that was to be in the midst of the crowd. Layla saw Delonté walking by and assumed he was looking for Nate. She grabbed his arm and he stopped.

"What's up, Delonté. You looking for your boy?"

"Hey Layla, Ms. Monique, and Yve. Don't y'all look good. Yeah, you seen him?" Delonté said while looking at Monique. He bent down and whispered in Layla's ear.

"What's up with Monique? She fucking or what?"

Layla almost spit out her drink. "Boy you are sick. Stop talking like that. Your boy is probably in the VIP room." Layla said while shoving Delonté away and laughing at his comment.

The girls got up and walked to the dance floor and started to get their groove on. Layla was in the zone and didn't notice Malachi walk up behind her. He stood behind her and was so turned on by her dancing that he felt his dick immediately stand at attention. None of the girls had yet to realize that Malachi was right there. Yve was dancing with some dude she met on the dance floor and Monique was also dancing with someone and too busy to notice Malachi as he stared at Layla.

Layla turned around and eyes were closed as she danced seductively to 50 Cent and Justin Timberlake song that was obviously designed for a stripper and had Layla rocking back and forth and swaying her hips and in the zone still with her eyes closed. When she opened her eyes, she was surprised to see Malachi standing in front of her but didn't stop dancing. She continued to give him a show and he moved closer to her so she could use his body as her pole. She did just that until the song came to an end.

"Damn, Layla. You really trying to give a nigga a heart attack, huh?" Malachi asked as he walked with Layla off the dance floor. Layla went straight to the bar and grabbed a napkin and wiped her forehead.

Layla gave Malachi a hug and the chemistry between the two was so thick that you could cut a knife with it. Malachi wanted badly to have Layla in the worse way but tried to remain cool under the circumstances. He could tell she was not the type to sleep around and all though he wouldn't think less of her if she surrendered to him, he found it sexy that she didn't even entertain the attraction he knew she also felt. Malachi asked Layla what she was drinking and she held up her almost empty flute. Rose Moët was her response and Malachi ordered another bottle and asked for a couple of more flutes. Levi walked in as if on cue when Monique and Yve were walking up. Yve and Layla gave each other a knowing look both thinking about the fact that Nate was still in the club. Monique immediately thanked Malachi and Levi for the beautiful watch she sported on her arm and they were happy to see she was grateful for a gift that they both considered small. Layla excused herself and said she would be back in a few. She went to the ladies room and looked in the mirror to check her make-up and to make sure her hair was in place. She then proceeded to the VIP room where she found Nate, Delonté, Al, and Nut popping bottles and having a good time. Layla gave Lyn a hug and invited her to hang with her and the girls if she didn't want to be around the fellas. Lyn thanked Layla for the offer but informed Layla that she was with Nut. Layla wasn't too surprised since she knew that Nut always admired Lyn from a distance. Layla was visibly irritated by the groupies that were also standing around in the guy's faces. However, to Nate's surprise, Layla acted real classy and spoke to everyone. Nate asked the cocktail waitress for another flute for Layla.

"Naw, I'm good. I have a bottle waiting for me at the bar. I just came to check on y'all but I see you all are doing quite fine." Layla winked at Nate, walked away, and out of the VIP room back to Malachi, Levi, and her friends.

The girls danced for another hour and all drank so much that they were feeling very nice and anyone on the outside looking in would say they were drunk. Malachi asked if they wanted to go get something to eat so the girls agreed and they all proceeded to walk out. Layla begin to text Nate out of respect to let him know she was leaving and that they were okay. Just as she was about to press the send button – Nate, Delonté, and Al were walking in their direction towards the door.

"Layla, come here," an obvious drunk Nate slurred.

The girls looked at one another and Layla excused herself so Nate wouldn't make a scene.

"Layla, are you alright?" Malachi asked with a concerned tone and look on his face.

"Yeah, I'm good. Why don't y'all go get the cars and I will meet y'all outside." Layla responded and begin walking towards Nate and his boys.

"Oh, so now you are free to talk?" Layla questioned Nate with her hand on her hip.

"Who the hell are those busters y'all over there talking to?" Nate questioned Layla while mugging Malachi and Levi.

"Just some friends. Why, who were all the groupies getting all that attention from y'all?" Layla asked not really caring.

"Oh, so it's tit for tat? Shawty, please don't make me have to hurt you in here." Nate said in a threatening tone, which let Layla know that he was definitely drunk and a little in his feelings.

"Look, I don't have time for this shit. Hit me tomorrow when you sober the hell up," Layla said through clenched teeth and walked away leaving them staring at her back.

"Yo, Nate, that was damn Malachi and his brother. How the hell do they know them?" Al commented as they stood in the foyer waiting for Delonté to stop talking to some female.

"Let's discuss this away from Delonté. No need of having to break bread with another motherfucker. This is business," Nate said and called for Delonté to hurry up and walked out the door to give the valet attendant his ticket.

The girls were following behind Malachi and Levi in Malachi's dark green Range Rover that would put any truck to shame. Monique was not happy about being the third wheel so she called her friend Carlos to see if he was out and about. It was perfect timing because he was just a block away at the *Zanzibar* night club which was also on the waterfront. Monique asked Yve to pull over so she could ride with Carlos and not be cramped in the back seat.

They ended up riding to *Steak in a Sac* in Oxon Hill, which was black owned and crowded with people who looked like they were fresh from the club. They waited for about twenty minutes before being seated. While they were waiting, Monique had already introduced Carlos to everyone.

Carlos was very handsome. He was light skin and tall with a goatee and seemed to be very into Monique by the way he was talking. He made comments like he wasn't letting her get away and things like that, which her girls found to be cute. He was also very sociable and got along well with Malachi and Levi. They all placed their orders and each couple was involved in their own side bar conversations.

"So, who was that nigga back at the club?" Malachi asked Layla.

"He's a good friend. I know it seemed kind of weird but he just had too much to drink." Layla responded.

"Yeah, it did but if you say you have it under control then I feel you but I don't need the drama, Layla. I got too much bullshit on my plate to be worrying about a damn jealous ass nigga."

Layla heard him but chose not to comment. She knew Nate could be a lot of things but a threat to Malachi wasn't one of them. Or was he?

"So, Carlos—Are you treating my girl right?" Yve asked Carlos breaking the side bar conversations that each of them were having.

"It's Yve, right? I think that is a question for Monique but I can tell you I definitely am trying my hardest."

"I know that's right." Yve said and winked at Monique.

The food arrived at the table and they all wasted no time in getting it in. Several minutes went by before anyone said anything.

"Damn, you can tell when black folks eatin' 'cause all talking cease," Levi said and started laughing. They all giggled off of that one but kept right on eating.

After a while, the waitress came back to the table and asked if anyone needed anything. They all said no and Malachi asked for the bill, which she reached in her black book to retrieve and handed it to him.

Carlos reached into his pocket to get money but Malachi insisted it was not worth them all breaking bills for since it was just something short. Layla was still thinking about how Nate disrespected her in front of Malachi in the club and became more furious by the minute.

Everyone got ready to leave and the girls were all saying goodnight but Levi had talked Yve into going with him to his house, which since she had never been was eager to see how Mr. GQ lived.

"Layla, can you drop Monique off and take my car? I will come get it tomorrow." Yve explained while looking in her purse for her keys.

"Sure," Layla said.

"Well, actually, Carlos is going to drop me off so Layla can just go straight home." Monique giggled and looked at Carlos with knowing eyes.

All eyes were now on Layla and Malachi.

"Damn, hoochies. Y'all just gonna leave me to fend for myself?" Layla joked while taking the keys from Yve.

"I will follow Layla home to make sure she gets there safely and y'all can go ahead and do y'all." Malachi said while giving dap to both his brother and then Carlos.

The girls hugged and each told the other to call first thing in the morning and they all walked out the restaurant and to their vehicles.

Malachi followed Layla home just as he said he would. When they pulled up, Layla got out of the car and went to sit in Malachi's truck. Malachi passed Layla the jay and he asked her if she was okay because she had a distant look in her eyes.

"Yeah, I'm good. Just can't believe I will finally be moving into my own place next week. I am so hyped but nervous as well." Layla admitted.

"Why are you nervous?" Malachi asked

"It will just be weird to finally leave the nest, I guess. But, it is really something that I need and badly want to do." Layla said while inhaling the jay and passing it back to Levi.

"Did you already pick out your furniture?"

"No, not yet. But actually, I need to do that and so much more. What are you doing tomorrow?" Layla asked.

"I need to be at the store for real since its Monday but can probably get Levi or one of our employees to cover. Why? Where are you trying to go?"

"I don't know—somewhere to get really nice furniture and accessories for my place." Layla was all smiles.

"I know just the place." Malachi said and tried to pass the jay back to Layla.

"Naw, I'm good. Actually, I'm sleepy so I'm going to head in. Thank you for following me home, Malachi. You know you really starting to grow on me, right?" Layla turned to Malachi and instantly felt the heat that radiated from both of their bodies.

Malachi didn't want to lose the moment, so he kissed her. Layla was mesmerized by how gentle he was and how his soft lips melted on hers. Layla started to pull herself away.

"Okay, seriously—we need to stop. Damn," was all Layla could say.

"Alright punk," Malachi said laughing at Layla's reaction. "Go ahead and get some sleep and we will hang out tomorrow."

"Bet." Layla said and jumped out of his truck and floated in the house. She was on cloud nine.

BABY G

Chapter 11

When Levi pulled up to his house, Yve was sleep. He pulled in the three car garage and got out the car and walked onto her side. Yve was not budging and didn't hear the car door shut or anything. Levi took this opportunity to prop the garage door open and to cut the alarm off. He went back and opened Yve's door. He slid her shoes off her feet and scooted her out of the car into his arms. Yve started to wake up but she was already in Levi's arms. She looked up at him, smiled and dozed right back off. Levi figured it was the drinks and food that had her in an almost comatose state. So, he walked her up the spiraling stair case and laid her in his bed.

He undressed her and put the covers over her. He then undressed himself placing his *Hermano* shirt and jeans in the hamper designated for the dry-cleaner and walked to the bathroom to take a shower.

While Levi was in the shower, Yve woke up to the sound of the water and to Levi humming. She sat up, stretched and looked around.

"Damn, this room is huge." Yve was not surprised to see how neat everything was. Levi was obviously a neat person. The bed was huge in its size and swallowed Yve. She was facing a fifty-two-inch plasma screen with speakers mounted in each corner of the room. The room was all white with a honey color theme. The bed was completely covered in white linen and the furniture was a nice light oak color that screamed expensive. The room was not cluttered by far and housed a sitting area in the far right side of the room with really nice furry white furniture that she was sure was real fur. There was a chandelier hanging over the glass coffee table that was in the sitting room. Yve got up and took her clothes off and opened the door to the bathroom. It was huge and filled with steam. Levi didn't notice her come in and much less open the door to the stand alone shower where he was still humming and lathered up with soap. He did, however, hear the door shut and turned around to what he thought was such a classy, beautiful lady. Yve took the rag from Levi hand and finished washing his body. His member didn't waste any time reacting to her touch. Yve then rinsed the rag out, soaped it again and washed her body off while Levi rinsed off. He turned around to watch her and she put her arms around his neck and started kissing him. You would have thought they have been lovers for years the way they intensely kissed. Yve broke the embrace, kneeled down to Levi's rock hard member and kissed the head of it with just as much intensity as she had kissed his mouth with. Levi was moaning and so turned on by her that he couldn't let her finish. He pulled her up and kissed her again and then stepped out the shower.

Yve was just as ready as he was so she turned the water off and followed him into his bedroom. Levi cut the lights off and turned on the fireplace with the remote that was sitting next to the bed. Levi went right to work. Licking and sucking all the water off Yve until she couldn't take anymore. She pulled him up and turned him over. She asked him for a condom and he pleaded with her with his eyes not to be serious. But, she was very serious. Not to destroy the moment, he reluctantly grabbed one from the top drawer of the nightstand beside the bed and placed it on. Yve helped him by rolling it the rest of the way on and then she bent down to kiss him on his neck and whispered, "I promise you won't know it's there," as she slowly sat on him.

Yve rode Levi like a pro and didn't stop until he exploded while calling her name. Yve was grateful that Levi's windows were covered so good that the dawn that had started to creep up, didn't shine in to the room.

Levi took the condom off, got up to dispose of it and scooted back in the bed. He kissed Yve and held her in his arms as they both instantly fell asleep.

When Yve woke up she realized she was in unfamiliar territory and for a minute, it didn't register to her where she was. She slowly eased out of bed and went to the bathroom to wash her face. She went back in the bedroom and grabbed her toothbrush out of her purse and looked over at Levi sleeping so peacefully. After Yve brushed her teeth, she headed out the room to explore Levi's house and to see what he had in the refrigerator so she could fix them something to eat. She peeked in the guest room to her left and noticed that it was empty and then across the hall to the other guest room, which Levi had set up as a complete office with a bookshelf and a huge mahogany desk, which sat a computer, printer and fax machine. She scanned his book case to see what books he had and she noticed he had a really nice collection of street novels and even her favorite, "The Coldest Winter Ever," by Sister Soulja. He also had a nice collection of biographies of different black influential leaders that she was impressed by.

Yve kept it moving and went down the spiral staircase. The house was carpeted with white Persian plush carpet, which she just loved walking barefoot on. It made her feel like she was walking on a cloud. When she got down stairs, she looked around only to find that he hadn't finished decorating, which was not a surprise since the house was so huge. He didn't bother to put anything but a huge artificial plant and a very nice dining table, which was solid wood and very expensive looking in the dining area and nothing was in the adjoining living room area. Yve walked in the kitchen and couldn't believe how huge it was. In the middle sat a huge granite island with black cabinets throughout the kitchen and stainless steel appliances. There was a sub-zero refrigerator and a stainless steel Movado wall clock was the only item that hung on the bare white walls. To say she was impressed was an understatement. She opened the fridge and couldn't believe how well stocked it was. She decided to fix some fried potatoes, turkey sausage, grits and toast. She was able to find everything she needed and was grateful that she didn't have to wake Levi up to ask where something was at. She fixed breakfast and placed everything on two plates for them and grabbed two paper towels and headed up the stairs. To Yve's surprise, Levi was awake watching ESPN.

"Good Morning Sweetie," Yve said while handing him his plate and giving him a peck on the lips.

"Damn Baby, this looks good. I can't even believe you are hungry again after eating early this morning." Levi commented while looking at how sexy Yve looked in his oversized t-shirt.

"Hungry is an understatement. Can you go get us something to drink?"

"Actually, there should be bottles of orange juice and water in the fridge on your side of the bed." Yve opened the fridge and grabbed two orange juices and handed Levi one.

"Thanks, beautiful." Levi said as he took the orange juice from Yve. Levi turned the television up with the remote and they both ate in silence.

"Let me find out you can throw down?" Levi said while putting his plate on the nightstand beside him. He grabbed Yve's plate after she took her last bite and placed it on top of his.

"What can I say, I got skills." Yve joked and gulped down her orange juice. Levi grabbed her and started tickling her, which caused her to almost spit out her orange juice. "Boy, stop playing." Yve was dying laughing when she placed her juice on the night stand from fear she would spill it if he didn't stop tickling her. "So you wanna play, do you?" Yve said jumping up to wrestle him. She jumped on him with intentions of holding his hands down but fell right in his face and they both started laughing hard and were stuck for a minute just looking at each other.

Yve kissed Levi and prepared herself for round two as she started kissing his body and working her way down to his machine gun that she couldn't wait to unload. She was kissing his stomach and then the crease of his waist until she found his member and held it in her hands with a look of lust in her eyes, it was evident that she wanted to swallow him whole. She kissed the head of his dick and took him in her mouth. Levi couldn't contain himself. Yve's mouth was so warm and wet that all he could do was moan.

"Damn Baby, suck your Boo." Was all Levi could muster up to say since Yve had started licking his shaft sensuously and like it was her last meal of her just started day. Yve loved feeling Levi's dick in her mouth. She knew that she was falling hard for him since she finally decided to take it to this level. She started sucking him real hard and deep throating him so that it would touch the back of her throat with every deep thrust. Levi couldn't take it anymore. He was about to explode and couldn't believe how fast she made him cum.

"Yes Yve, suck this dick baby. You about to make that dick bust all over you." Levi said as he hurried up and pulled his dick out of Yve's mouth all the while trying not to nut on the bed sheets but Yve wasn't having it and made him cum all over her mouth while she caught it and spit it out all over his dick, which turned Levi on even more. She continued to suck and spit for a little while until she was sure she got it all. Then she got up and went to the bathroom and grabbed a wash cloth and ran steamy hot water on it. She grabbed the mouth wash from off the sink took a swig, gargled, spit it out and walked back into the bedroom to wipe Levi's dick off. To her surprise, he was still hard as a brick. Levi motioned for Yve to turn around and he entered her wet pussy and she did as she was told and prepared herself for round three.

BABY G

Chapter 12

Layla woke up first thing in the morning and jumped in the shower and got dressed. She first called Yve to see what she wanted her to do about her car but she kept getting her voicemail.

"I know damn well this girl see me calling her." Layla mumbled.

She left Yve a message letting her know her car would be in front of her folks house with her keys under the mat. About an hour later, Layla was dressed and hopping in Malachi's truck.

"Hi Malachi." Layla greeted him and got comfortable in his leather seats.

Malachi responded by leaning over and giving her a kiss, starting off where they finished last night. He couldn't help how well put together she was for first thing in the morning. Layla had on some stretch skinny *Joe's* jeans and a *BEBE* shirt with the matching tennis shoes. Layla sat back in the plush leather seats, grabbed Malachi's iPod, and started searching for songs to play.

"So, where are we going?" Layla asked.

"There is a nice furniture store off of 95 between Baltimore and Delaware I want to take you to." Malachi responded and looked at Layla.

"Cool. Can we grab something to eat first?" Layla asked while selecting Donnie McClurklin's, *We fall down*, from the iPod.

"Sure we can." Malachi was surprised at Layla's choice of songs and admired her even more if that were possible.

"Do you have a relationship with God?" Layla asked Malachi.

"Yes, I do. I pray and I know that all the material things I have can be gone at the blink of an eye. What about you?" Malachi was glad she asked and felt it was good to know that she actually wanted to get to know him.

"Yes, I have a relationship with Jesus. I'm the first to admit that it could be better but I love the Lord. I was raised in church and I believe that it's true that if you train up a child in the way that he or she should go, that they shall not depart. I know that I can be a better person and so that is why I will not stop going to church or just totally give up. Eventually the time will come when I can't do anything else but fully serve the Lord. I just pray He doesn't come back before I totally give myself to Him." Layla explained and turned away to look out the window.

They both sat deep in thought. Malachi couldn't help to think about how real Layla was. It was so rare in the women in this area to be so wise and at such a young age. He truly wanted her to be his.

They arrived at the Waffle House which happened to be a couple of exits from the furniture store that Malachi wanted to take Layla too. They ordered waffles, chicken, grits, and eggs. Layla thought the food was so good especially considering it was a little small and kind of run down.

After they finished eating, they hopped on the road to the furniture store.

Monique was up at the crack of dawn because she had a client coming over and knew she wouldn't have time to fix anything to eat while she was doing hair so she started early with Carlos still asleep. She fixed fried potatoes, eggs, grits, and smoked sausages. Carlos couldn't help but wake up after smelling the food. Monique came in the room just as he was waking up.

"Good Morning, sleepy head." She giggled. "There is a new toothbrush on the sink in the bathroom. I have a client coming over shortly so I got up to fix you breakfast."

"Thank you, Baby. You didn't have to do that." Carlos responded while getting up and going to the bathroom down the hall.

"How long will you be doing hair?" Carlos yelled down the hall.

"I should be finished no later than one o'clock. Why what's up?"

"I was thinking we could go to the mall together this time." Carlos laughed as he came out the bathroom. He grabbed Monique and gave her a kiss.

"Sure that's cool. Make yourself at home and fix your plate and I am going to straighten up a little and prepare for my client." Monique said while grabbing a sheet out the closet and placing it on the floor. She then placed a chair on top of the sheet.

Carlos did as he was told and fixed himself a plate and went back in Monique's bedroom. Not even five minutes passed before Monique's client came knocking at the door. Monique led her into the living room and instructed her to take a seat in the chair. She took the hair the girl gave her and cut the pack open and gave her some and showed her how much to break off to pass to her. Carlos was fully dressed and brought his plate into the kitchen. He kissed Monique and told her he was going to change and would be back around three o'clock to get her. Monique was all smiles as he walked out the door.

When Layla and Malachi walked in the furniture store, the sales people were on them. Malachi instructed them that they would find one of them if and when they found something that they liked so they could lay off. Layla loved the furniture store Malachi brought her to. It had very nice modern and traditional furniture with so many different options to choose from. The store was two levels so they took their time checking out every inch of the store. Layla saw a bedroom set with big marble post that she set her eyes on. The set was a dark oak with pink and white marble post on all four ends. The same marble coloring covered the dresser, night stand, and armoire. Layla fell in love with it. It would easily set her back eight thousand dollars if she decided to purchase it but she brought fifteen thousand out prepared to furnish her entire condo. Malachi saw that she really liked the set she was looking at because it was the only one that she actually stayed at longer than five minutes. He loved her eye for style because it was indeed hot. He told her he thought she should purchase it. Layla took in his comment and grabbed his arm so they could continue walking. She took Malachi to the living room furniture sets and scrolled around until she stopped at a pink leather coach set.

"Damn, this is the bomb." Layla screamed. "I have never seen a pink leather sofa and love seat before."

She loved the fact that the set came with a chaise. Malachi loved her excitement and thought it too was hot since it was different. He loved that she was definitely thinking outside the box and could see her hooking the look up. Layla started sitting on the sofa and lounging trying to get a feel of how comfortable it was. She felt like the leather felt better than Malachi's Rover seats. She was sold until she looked at each price. The sofa by itself was four thousand dollars.

"Oh, hell no. Who spends this kind of money on a damn couch?" Layla asked to no one in particular. "Okay, let's keep it moving because this is just ridiculous."

Malachi and Layla continued to walk around the store. Layla was ready to decide on her purchase. "Malachi, can you get one of the sales people for me?" Malachi walked off and left Layla to do as he was asked.

Layla was disturbed because she hadn't found a living room set she liked besides the leather set which she knew she couldn't afford. Malachi returned with a woman named, Iza. Layla guessed that she was a Hispanic woman in her late forties. She was well dressed and greeted Layla with the utmost respect.

She extended her hand to Layla. "Hello, my name is Iza. How can I assist you on today?" The lady spoke with a heavy accent.

"Hi Iza, my name is Layla, and I would like to know whether a particular bedroom set is in stock." Layla said while shaking Iza's hand.

"Well, let's go over and see the set that has caught your eye Ms. Layla."

Layla led the way towards the oak poster bedroom set that grabbed her attention. When they reached the set, Layla explained that she wanted a queen-size bed and all of the accessories including the armoire. She also told Iza she was interested in an extra night stand. Iza scanned everything with a gadget she was holding and informed Layla that it was all in stock. Malachi asked Iza if Mr. Rodriguez was in today. She informed him that he was and she walked away to retrieve him.

"Who is Mr. Rodriguez?" Layla asked Malachi.

"He is the owner." Malachi stated nonchalantly.

"Mr. Walters." An older Hispanic man came over and Malachi embraced him in a brotherly hug.

"Long time no see. *Como estas el hermano*?" Mr. Rodriguez inquired on Levi's well doing.

"He is fine. He sends his regards." Malachi responded. "This is my friend Layla. Layla, this is Mr. Rodriguez."

"Awww, Ms. Layla. *Muy Bonita*. How are you?" Layla giggled because she too knew a little Spanish and knew that he just said she looked very pretty or something to that effect.

"Hello. Nice to meet you and thank you." The two men both looked at one another and Malachi winked at Mr. Rodriguez.

"So, what brings you all this way? New house?" Mr. Rodriguez asked Malachi.

Malachi laughed and shook his head no. "Not by far. Layla here is looking for furniture and is interested in this bedroom set along with the pink leather sofa set upstairs." Iza was smiling so hard no doubt counting her commission if Layla actually purchased both.

"I see." Mr. Rodriguez smiled and looked at Layla. "Well, let's go talk my man. Iza, please write up a ticket for everything Ms. Layla want and bring her and the ticket into my office when you're done."

"*Si, Senor*." Iza responded and started writing up everything.

Malachi and Mr. Rodriguez walked away and into Mr. Rodriguez' office. When Iza walked Layla into Mr.

Rodriguez' office the two men were laughing and Mr. Rodriguez welcomed Layla in.

"Ms. Layla, have a seat." Mr. Rodriguez said while pointing at the seat next to Malachi. Iza handed Mr. Rodriguez the ticket for Layla's furniture selections and excused herself.

"Well Ms. Layla, I see you have chosen some really nice items from my store that don't sell as well as some of my other less expensive items." The older man was rubbing his chin while speaking to Layla.

"Yes, they are really nice items but I am not prepared nor can I afford to pay almost eighteen thousand dollars for furniture that will only be in a place I am leasing. So, I really will just settle for the bedroom furniture and be happy with that." Malachi smiled at Layla and patted her leg which he was trying to hint to her to slow down.

"Ms. Layla, Mr. Walters here is a really good customer of mine and so is his brother. I can give you twenty percent off of everything you want." Mr. Rodriguez said and pulled out a calculator.

After he was finished ringing up everything, to Layla's surprise it ended up being a little under fifteen grand. Layla was ecstatic. She jumped right on it, paid Mr. Rodriguez in cash and made arrangements for her furniture to be delivered to her condo the upcoming Friday which was her move in date. Malachi and Mr. Rodriguez shook hands, Malachi thanked him for such a generous deal, and the two left and headed home.

On the ride home, Layla couldn't stop thanking Malachi for working out the deal on her behalf. Malachi sparked up a jay and the two enjoyed their high. It was still early so Layla wasn't ready to leave Malachi just left.

"So, what do you have planned the rest of the day?" Layla inquired.

"I have to close up the shop tonight so I will most likely be at the store until about ten o'clock." Malachi responded and looked at Layla.

"Oh, okay. Maybe I can see you later?" Layla took the jay from Malachi inhaled and tried not to look at him. She feared her face would tell how she felt, because she was indeed ready to take it to the next level with Malachi.

"No problem. That's a bet. I will pick you up when I'm done and we can hang out, or we can go to one of my places." Malachi responded. The two set in silence the remainder of the ride home. Malachi dropped Layla off at her house and they gave each other a nice long kiss.

"See you later."

That was music to Layla's ears as she headed in the house on cloud nine.

BABY G

Chapter 13

Malachi entered the shop and Levi greeted him. "What's up, Bro?" Levi gave him a brotherly hug and dap.

"Ain't nothing, just left from taking Layla to see Mr. Rodriguez so she can furnish her place. He told me to tell you hello." Malachi said and walked to the register.

There were a few Howard University students looking around the store.

"Oh, yeah. How that old pimp doing?" Levi asked laughing.

"He's good. He just made a quick fourteen thousand off of Layla so I'd say he's doing damn good."

"Word? Shawty rolling like that?" Levi asked. "I actually dropped Yve to her car this morning which was parked at Layla's crib."

"Man, she is thorough. I'm digging her. She might just be Mrs. Walter but I have to do something about Angel. Her ass will not move out." Malachi said with conviction in his voice.

"You haven't told Layla about Angel yet?" Levi asked already knowing the answer.

127

"Naw, man. I don't want her to start faking. Especially when Angel has one foot out the door. If I could push the other one out, I would've, but you know I got too much love for Nashiya to do that." Malachi was rubbing his head.

He printed out the receipts from the day and ran a weekly summary and walked to their office in the back. Malachi was always concerned about Angel's daughter, Nashiya. She was seven-years-old and meant the world to him. Him and Angel had been together for three years and had been enemies for the last year. She did her thing and he did his. He allowed her and Nashiya to stay in the house that he purchased only because Angel was still in school. He wanted Nashiya to have a stable home so he put up with Angel based on that. However, he had already purchased a two bedroom condo not far from Georgetown so Angel could easily get back and forth. He was just looking for the right moment to tell her that it was seriously time to call it quits. They never had sex any more, not that Angel didn't want it. She wanted the luxuries of being with Malachi but she wasn't in love with him and vice versa. Malachi decided that he would tell her that night when he got home. He called Layla and cancelled plans with her. She sounded a little irritated but he let that ride. Malachi spent the reminder of the day in the store handling business.

Nate and Al were at Nate's apartment going over the plan for that evening and getting dressed. It was understood that they wouldn't use their weapons unless they absolutely had to. They were ready to make the move and sit outside of Lashone's house and wait for the lame buster to appear. They were able to get a rent-a-rock car from a crack head that wouldn't be able to be traced back to them. The crack head was already so stoned that he wouldn't be able to point them out if his life depended on it. Although they were certain that it wouldn't come to that.

Nate picked up the phone to call Layla. The one person he felt he could trust. To his surprise, she picked up on the first ring.

"Hello?" Layla answered.

"What's up, Baby G?" Nate spoke.

"Nigga, please. Are you calling to apologize for tripping the other night?" Layla said while smacking her lips loud enough for Nate to understand that she was clearly still upset for his episode in the club.

"Damn, okay. My bad for getting out of line. You just do that to me." Nate said in a sexy tone. He always knew just how to melt Layla. "But look, enough of that, I'm just calling you so you will be on point just in case I need you to bail me out if something go down tonight."

"What the hell are you talking about? What are you up to, Nate?" Layla yelled through the phone.

Her heart was beating quickly and just the thought of something happening to Nate made her sick to her stomach.

"Calm down, Shawty. Look, nothing will happen but just in case, I wanted to put you on point. You got money stashed, right, or do I need to bring you some?" Nate was getting irritated but understood how much Layla really cared and possibly loved him.

"Yeah, Babe. I got you." That was all Layla could say.

She was so tired of the emotions she was feeling. She felt like Nate needed to step up to the plate before she possibly let Malachi do what he couldn't.

"Alright, that's my Baby G. I will hit you late tonight. Okay?"

"Yeah, alright. Nate, please be safe, Boo."

"I got you Layla, I'm good." Was all Nate said before hanging up the phone. Layla sat on the other end of the phone confused by the conversation she just had with him. She was scared for some reason and she didn't know why. She had a bad feeling and just couldn't shake it.

It was three o'clock and Monique was dressed and waiting on Carlos to come over. She was really digging him. He had just called and said he would be there in just a few minutes. Monique had on a *Juicy Couture* sweat suit and wore her hair in a bushy ponytail with a peach ribbon tied around it, which matched her sweat suit. She only wore eyeliner and lip gloss that accented her big eyes and her sexy lips. Carlos knocked on the door. Monique opened it and he greeted her with a kiss.

"You ready?" Carlos asked.

"Yeah, let me grab my purse." Monique walked in the back to her bedroom and grabbed her purse just as her cell phone started ringing.

"Hey Chica, what's up?"

"Hey girl, ain't nothing." Monique responded to Layla. "About to go to the mall with Carlos. What's up with you?"

"I was calling to tell you about the furniture I just bought for my condo. You not going to believe what color my couch is but you being you, you will appreciate this."

"What color is it, Layla? I sure hope you didn't go overboard." Monique laughed.

"It's pink!" Layla yelled.

"Layla, what the heck are you going to do with a pink couch? First of all, your butt is not the prissy type so why would you go and buy a pink couch?"

Carlos walked in the room and Monique gave him a wink and walked out behind him. They left out the apartment and Monique locked her front door.

"Be quiet. Wait until you see it. It is so nice and so comfortable. You know I am going to need you to help me decorate so start thinking of some colors that will go with pink."

"Okay, I got you. How much did you spend on furniture, 'cause I know you." Monique really was the mother out of the crew and it tickled Layla.

"Mother, you honestly don't want to know. But tell Carlos I said what's up and enjoy your day shopping. Don't forget to get me something. Bye" Layla said and hung up the phone before Monique could say anything or rather ask her about the cost of her furniture again.

Carlos and Monique were in the car and on the way to the mall. Carlos drove a nice new fully loaded S Class Benz. It was navy blue with tinted windows and nice rims. Carlos and Monique talked the entire ride. Monique opened up and told Carlos about her mom and how she came to be on her own. He expressed sympathy and also told her about his rough upbringing in the roughest hood in Southeast, Berry Farms. He told her how he hustled growing up and stopped when he reached his goal to put himself through trade school to become an electrician. Monique was all ears and was impressed that he actually accomplished what so many young black men his age couldn't. She always thought there were only two ways to get out of the game, jail or a body bag. Monique told Carlos she was proud of him, which caused him to blush. Next thing she knew they were pulling into the parking lot of White Flint Mall. They parked and walked into the mall.

They first stopped in Foot Locker and Carlos purchased some fresh Nike's and some white tees. He picked out some cute Nike's for Monique. She was glad because she rarely purchased tennis shoes and had no idea what was considered in style. They walked the mall until they both were tired of walking. Monique had so many shopping bags, she couldn't hold them all. Carlos had to purchase one of those stroller carts that are normally used for people with kids. Monique enjoyed being pampered for a change.

"You hungry?" Carlos asked.

"Yes, I can definitely put something on my stomach. What do you have the taste for?" Monique asked just as Carlos phone was ringing. He answered the call and ended it just as fast.

"Umm, let's do PF Chang." He suggested and nudged her in the direction of the restaurant. When they were seated and had ordered, Carlos asked Monique would she join him at an all-white party which was a few weeks away. Monique was all smiles and loved that he wasn't one of those men that felt he couldn't party with a female. She happily accepted and was all smiles the rest of the meal. Her mind immediately started working overtime to think of the perfect outfit to wear. She already put two and two together and figured this was the same party that Yve had told them about. She made a mental note to make sure they all went shopping together for their outfits.

BABY G

Chapter 14

Nate and Al were now sitting outside of Lashone's house waiting on the nigga to leave so they could follow him. They were in the driveway of someone's home a few houses up and were smoking a jay passing time.

"He's leaving now." Al said and started the car up. Nate had his pistol sitting on his lap and another tucked in his sock on his left leg.

"Alright, so just let him turn the corner before you pull out the drive way." Nate instructed.

They got comfortable in the car because they knew the next couple of hours would be extremely long since it was only six o'clock and still light outside. Thankfully the dude's next stop was to meet up with his crew so Nate and Al laid low waiting for them to leave from out of the beat up houses in the projects that neither of them was quite comfortable with and it showed because both kept their pistols in ready mode on their laps.

Hours later, the dudes walked out. It was important for Nate and Al to know where they kicked it at so if anything went wrong, they would know where to find them. Nate and Al decided not to follow them to the store since they were fully aware of where they would end up at. So, they slouched down in their car and let the truck of dudes ride past them before starting up their engine and leaving.

It was close to midnight and the dudes were just getting to the store. Nate and Al were parked about a block up ready and waiting. It was four young dudes total and they obviously thought this was going to be a quick hit which Nate rationalized was the reason behind none of them visibly holding any weapons from the angle that him and Al were watching from. Their plan was to wait for them to come out and catch them by surprise. Nate and Al jumped out the car, pulled their ski mask down over their faces and ran towards the store. Just as they were reaching the store, the dudes were coming out. Nate yelled for them to stop and freeze. From the look of it, they thought they were the police at first and did just what they were told. When they noticed it was stick up boys, one of them grabbed for his Glock and immediately Al shot at him hitting him in his arm. The young dude dropped the gun and fell on his knees. Nate snatched the duffle bag from one of the dudes and instructed them all to go back in the store. As soon as they walked back in the store, Nate and Al turned and ran towards their get-away car. The dudes followed suit and were popping off in their direction. They heard sirens from a far and high tailed down Georgia Avenue not looking back.

Nate and Al pulled up to Al's house around the way after ditching the get-away ride. He lived in the basement of his folk's house so they used the back entrance. Both were on a super adrenaline high. Nate was the first to speak.

"You good, main man?" Nate asked Al. "Look, fuck that shit. You did what you had to do. Man, homeboy just got a wounded arm. He good."

"Oh for sure. I'm good." Al said not sounding convincing. "Let's count up this dough and see what we made off with." Al said while throwing the bag on his coffee table and rubbing his palms together.

"Damn!" they both shouted in unison.

Nate had grabbed the bag and emptied its contents. They both stood in awe looking at what Nate easily guesstimated to be close to a half million dollars in cash, four pounds of heroin, and six keys of cocaine.

"They are really getting it." Nate said. "Damn, this a good jump off."

"Yeah, but with work like this, they gonna be sweating niggas to see who coming up." Al stated.

"Yeah, and that's why we will lay low and not change our normal routine. Think about it, only the two of us know about this. I can easily get rid of the keys by selling it for dirt cheap to the little slangers around the way. They will be so happy to get it that I doubt questions be asked."

"True. But, just hold off until we hear what the word on the street is. Until then we can keep this locked up here. Let's divide the money, stash this, and go for a drink. I can definitely use one, my nigga." Al said shaking his head.

"Yeah, me too bro."

It was about two o'clock in the morning and Layla was still up trying to fall asleep. She had tried calling Nate's phone several times only to keep getting his voicemail on the first ring. She finally decided to try one more time before completely losing her mind and start calling police stations. To her surprise, he picked up on the first ring.

"Yo, what's up Baby?" Nate answered.

"You, what's up? How the hell you gonna ask me what's up? Why the hell didn't you call me 'cause I know you got my messages. You got me over here sweating bullets, worried about your ass." Layla was highly upset and started going on Nate as soon as he answered.

"Slow down Baby G, I'm good. Yo, Al – swing past Layla's house and pick her up. Baby, be outside in five minutes. We about to get drinks and scoop you up." Nate told Layla and hung up before waiting for her to respond.

"Man, I know you are not about to tell Layla what went down?" Al asked. Al was visibly a little nervous. He knew Layla and Nate were close but he also knew that rather Nate wanted to admit it or not – seeing her with Malachi the other night was not cool.

"Naw, I meant what I said – only the two of us know and I want to keep it like that. So, stop tripping. I just need Layla to know I'm good. You know that's my heart."

"Alright, Nigga. Don't be getting all sappy and shit. Just wanted to make sure you wasn't going to considering she know the nigga and all." Al stated as they pulled up to Layla's house.

Nate tried ignoring Al's comments but deep down, he had been wondering what was the extent of Layla's and Malachi's relationship since he saw the two at the club the other night. Nate was dialing Layla's phone but she was already on her way out the door. She had on a pink juicy couture sweat suit and all white air force ones with her hair in a wild ponytail. She had only lip gloss on and to Nate she looked perfect, flawless. He loved it when she didn't wear make-up. He hated seeing woman with all that shit on their face.

"I can't believe you had me calling you all night and you ain't answer the damn phone." Layla started soon as she got in the truck. The thoughts he had went right out the window soon as she opened her mouth and got in.

He chuckled to himself. *Gotta love her, he thought.*

"Where we going this late? Ain't shit open but legs and maybe the liquor store. Layla said, cracking a smile.

She reached up the front around the back of the passenger seat and gave Nate a much needed embrace. She loved him dearly and wouldn't know what to do if something was to happen to him. He kissed her hand and acknowledged her as only he could.

They decided on the Greenbelt Marriott's Blue Sky Bar to unwind and get a few drinks. There were a handful of hotel guest sitting at various tables and several more people sitting around the bar. The bar was a blue lit bar with two pool tables in the back for guest to enjoy. The bartender greeted them as soon as they sat down. Layla ordered a Remy Side Car with a sugar rim and both Nate and Al ordered Ciroc and lime juice.

"So, what the hell you two do tonight?" Layla asked while stirring at both of them trying to read their reactions.

"Yo, chill Layla. All you need to know is that I'm okay. You know I would never incriminate myself." Nate said laughing trying to lighten up the mood.

"Incriminate, Nigga – I'm supposed to be your ride or die and you can't tell me what the hell had me up all night worrying whether I was going to have to bail you out of jail or some shit? You are truly unbelievable." Layla said and rolled her eyes at both of them.

"Look here, I know you got my back Shawty so just chill." Nate put his arm around Layla's waist and pulled her closer to him. "I got you too Babe and trust me – you have nothing to worry about." Nate whispered in Layla's ear.

Layla decided to just let the subject go and enjoy being around Nate which is something she hadn't done in a while.

"Hey, let's go shoot pool." Al said getting off his stool.

"Alright, I'm in. I got one hundred dollars I beat you." Layla said pulling out a bill.

"Bet!" Al said pulling out his money. They both gave Nate their money who was shaking his head. "Baby G" always ready," Nate said laughing.

"Be quiet, Nate." Layla said smiling and grabbing for a stick.

"Al, I don't know why you took that bet like she is not gonna whip that ass." Nate said sitting on a bar stool next to the pool table.

"Don't tell him nothing, I got this – Boo." Layla said breaking the balls.

They were having a good ole time and both the guys were not letting the events of earlier that night linger any longer on their minds. Layla ended up beating Al bad. He had four balls still left on the table when she knocked the eight ball in.

"Game, nigga! Never bet against a lady. We only let y'all win on rare occasions. We are good at everything." Layla said getting her money from Nate.

"You silly as shit, Girl." Al said giving Layla dap. "It's your world. I'm going to get us another round." Al said walking to the bar.

"Come here," Nate said pulling Layla between his legs. "Damn, I kind of missed you," he told her while cupping her butt.

"If that's your way of telling me you miss me, Nate – I miss you too." Layla said and gave Nate a kiss. Layla's juices were starting to flow and she realized just how much she actually missed Nate.

"After this drink let's go to your place since we right around the corner." Layla said while caressing Nate's chest.

"What about Al, then again – forget I asked. His ass can take my truck or just crash in the living room." Nate said.

Al brought them back their drinks and they sat around and kicked it until they finished. Nate closed out the bill and they headed to the truck.

"Yo, Al – you can drop Layla and me off and take the truck and come back in the morning or just chill over my place." Nate said as they got in the truck.

Since Al still had the keys, he jumped in the driver seat and they drove off. Al grabbed the jay that was in the ash tray and sparked it.

"Yo, I can chill at your place cause I'm damn sure not gonna feel like coming all the way back in the morning? Layla, you gonna cook us some breakfast in the morning?" Al asked while looking in his rearview mirror at her.

"I will think about it nigga. I need to find your ass a girlfriend. You're not gonna be using my skills." Layla said jokingly.

By the time they made their way in Nate's apartment, they were all buzzing. Nate and Layla walked in first took of their shoes and headed straight to the bedroom. Al, followed suit taking his shoes off and went to the bathroom before flopping down on the couch and dozing off.

In the room, Layla flopped down on the bed. She started taking her sweat suit off but Nate came over to where she was and started helping. So, she stopped and allowed him to finish undressing her.

"Baby, you really had me worried tonight." Layla said while looking directly into Nate's eyes. "I really would be devastated if something was to happen to you." Layla tried her best to fight away the tears that were threatening to come out.

"Baby G, I got this. Can you please not worry your little self? I need to know that I can count on you Layla. So, you have to be strong in certain circumstances and try to brush the worry off so you can think clearly at all times. You feel me?" Nate said and started kissing Layla.

"Yeah, I'm definitely feeling you. Even more so when you give me what's mine." Layla said grabbing Li'l Nate out his pants as he climbed out of them and his boxers while inching on top of her. They slowly made love, both with different thoughts on their minds. Layla wondering if their relationship would ever go further and Nate thinking about how long he would have to lay low before making it official with Layla.

BABY G

Chapter 15

Malchai walked in his house which was fit for a king. He had a mini-mansion built in Potomac, Maryland which was about forty-five minutes to an hour from the store. Far enough so that he would always know if he was being tailed and close enough to the city. Plus, he enjoyed the long drive which gave him a chance to clear his mind. He could hear Angel and Nashiya in the kitchen so he strolled in there in anticipation of finally getting some things off his chest.

"Hi Nay." Malachi yelled when he walked in the kitchen.

Nashiya ran up to him and gave him a hug. They had a relationship as if they were biologically connected. Angel was sitting on one of the stools at the breakfast bar eating a slice of cheese cake. He would wonder how she kept her perfect figure but then he didn't have to considering she had a personal trainer that trained her three times a week in their home gym that he was sure he was footing the bill for.

"Hi to you too." Angel said to Malachi.

He walked to the refrigerator and got a bottle of water before responding.

"Hi Angel. Nay, go to your room or to the theatre so your mom and I can talk." Nashiya did as she was told and ran upstairs to her room. Malachi studied Angel and admired how beautiful she was. She was Puerto Rican and black and was absolutely gorgeous but that no longer kept him interested. He needed more. She was a little green, but of course, that was a good and bad thing.

"Come sit down, Papi." Angel said trying to lighten the mood. "How was your day? I called you like three times and you didn't answer. What *puta* you were with today?" Angel said while rolling her eyes as Malachi sat across from her at the bar.

"See, that's your problem. You always think I have something going on with a female. I was taking care of business. You know, keeping this mortgage paid and shit. Angel – I'm just gonna get straight to the point – we need to stop playing games with each other. It's been months since we slept together and I'm just not in love with you anymore. I know regardless of what you say now, you are not in love with me either. You like the benefits of our arrangement." Malachi said, looking straight in Angel's eyes. He could see her eyes getting watery and prepared himself for the drama he knew was going to unfold.

"What the hell are you saying, Malachi? Your ass is unbelievable. You think your shit don't stink? So, what about my classes and where the hell are we supposed to go? Do you recall I left all my family behind to follow your ass down here?" Angel was upset and Malachi knew she would be but she was just concerned about keeping her luxury lifestyle together.

"Look, I am not gonna leave you hanging. I got you a condo right near Georgetown campus so you can finish taking your classes, and I will put enough money in your account to make sure you get your degree here or up top if you decide to go back home. You know I love you and Nashiya. Shit just ain't working out and it's time for us to be real with each other."

Angel was now sobbing uncontrollably but started to relax once she heard him say that he loved them.

"So, we just gonna go our separate ways just like that?" Angel cried trying not to look at him.

"Baby, come here." Malachi reached across the table for Angel's hand and led her around the bar. She stood in between his legs.

"You know you will always have a piece of my heart and if you or Nashiya ever need anything, you know I'm just a phone call away, right?"

"That's if you answer your phone." Angel said and tried cracking a smile. "So, where exactly is my new condo? And who's footing the bill for it? You know I can't get a job as demanding as my classes are, Chi."

Angel had her hands on her hips and was waiting for an answer. Angel always called Malachi by the end of his name when she wanted something. Angel only had two more semesters to go before getting her Doctorate of Medicine Degree. She was definitely a grinder and he admired that she was smart enough to put his money to good use while they were together. Although she blew enough of it too. Angel had every piece of clothing, jewelry, and handbag imaginable. She absolutely wanted for nothing. Malachi was sure she was smart enough to have an account on the side that he knew nothing about.

"Look, I will take care of everything. I'm tired of hearing about this shit. Why don't you go get Nay ready for bed and let's try enjoying tonight. I arranged to have movers come pack your stuff and everything so you won't have to lift a finger. You know I miss the way you deep throat this dick, right?" Malachi said with his hands on his crotch. Angel was a freak for real and he knew that she missed sexing him so he was about to definitely blow her back out cause once she moved out, he decided there was no going back.

"Mami, got you Papi," Angel said licking her glossed lips and sashaying her big ass out the kitchen.

Malachi was satisfied with the results of their conversation and now was thinking of how he was going to get Layla on his team full time. He figured, the house wouldn't appeal to her like that since she was raised in a nice home. He knew she would be impressed but since she was moving into her own condo, he couldn't just keep her spending the night like most woman that was on money. The moment any of his former women came to any of his places in the past, they ended up getting comfortable and just staying until he was ready for their ass to leave. He knew he had to approach her in a different way.

Malachi grabbed the bottle of Ciroc and got two glasses of ice and went to his bedroom. Angel was still in Nay's room so he put the bottle and glasses on the nightstand and headed to the bathroom to take a shower. He started thinking about how long of a day he had. The store had been pretty busy but normally all Saturdays were. Malachi made a mental note to go and move the work they had stashed at the store over to one of his safe houses. Since they sold weight, they definitely didn't keep a lot of niggas around them and only dealt with a handful of niggas that were loyal and respected the game and their position. He made sure they knew that if they wanted to do business with them, it was on their terms and they were never by no means to discuss who their connect was. The good thing about DC is that there were only a certain amount of niggas getting money on a serious level and since niggas were so territorial, it made it easy to only have to supply a handful. Malachi decided to deal with business tomorrow and enjoy the remainder of his evening with Angel. He turned on the flat-screen that was in the bathroom to ESPN and caught up on the games he missed. He decided he would take Layla to the next game that was worth seeing. He couldn't believe how Layla consumed his mind. He couldn't wait to feel her insides. He knew it would be good. She looks green in that department so he could certainly teach her some new things he thought.

He turned the water off and dried off his body. He put a little cologne on and headed in the bedroom in nothing but his birthday suit. When he walked into the room, to his surprise Angel had candles set up throughout the room and music playing in the background. It sounded like his old Twelve-Play CD. He smiled to himself and looked around for Angel. He didn't see her so he fixed himself a drink and made himself comfortable on his King sized bed. He noticed a sheet of paper on his pillow, so he grabbed it and opened it up and begin reading.

"Papi,

I have something special planned for you tonight. If you really think you can forget me that easily, I plan On making it extremely hard. Give me twenty more minutes and I will be up. Just put in one of your many "flicks" and wait Patiently for my return."

Wifey 4 Life

Malachi was speechless because Angel never really did sporadic things. He normally initiated their sex but once he got her started, it was hard to stop her. She was beyond nasty and took it any way he gave it to her. He got up off the bed and put in one of his DVD's and poured himself a hefty shot and downed it. His dick was already hard so he was ready. He started watching the porno and before he knew it, he was beating his meat. He grabbed tissue off his night stand when he felt himself about to explode and released himself in the tissue. He heard Angel walking through the hall. He positioned himself in the middle of his bed, ready for her to take control. He was glad he got the first one out the way so he could enjoy every minute of their final night. Angel walked in the room with a trench coat on and red heels. She stood in front of his bed and slowly removed the coat displaying a red sheer teddy. She then walked to the bed, grabbed the remote and turned the television off.

"We're making our own movie tonight, Papi." Angel seductively crawled up the bed and took a scarf out the night stand beside the bed and tied it around Malachi's eyes. He immediately protested but gave in when she nibbled on his ear and whispered.

"Let me take control, Chi. I got this." was all he heard as she took him in her mouth. Malachi senses were all aware and he heard the bedroom door squeak.

"Yo, is that Nay – Angel." He asked while waiting for Angel to stop and do something.

Instead he felt her shake her head no and he decided to just lay back and enjoy her. Next thing he knew, the blindfold was being taken off of him. With the candles shining all through the room, he was able to make out a beautiful black women standing next to the bed.

"Damn." Malachi said and looked down at Angel. She might not have to go anywhere is all he thought as Angel came up from below and started kissing him. He grabbed her ready for her to sit on him but Angel stopped him and told him with her finger that it wasn't time. Instead, she pulled him up and invited the girl to sit down on the bed and the two put on a show for him. The girl, who Angel

informed him was to be called Ms. Nice, did a better job
than he ever could. He was enjoying the show but his
body was letting him know that he needed to jump in
immediately. He smacked Ms. Nice on her ass and she
turned around and grabbed his dick. She put all nine
inches in her mouth. Angel was getting jealous so
Malachi positioned her so he could finish what Ms. Nice
was doing. Angel was reaching her climax and started
speaking in Spanish which she often did when she came.
Malachi asked Angel to turn around and entered her ass
while Ms. Nice went to lie in front of Angel. To his
surprise, Angel started licking her as best she could in
between of Malachi banging her out. Malachi was finally
ready to cum so he pulled out of Angel and came all over
her back. Angel and Malachi both collapsed and lay down
on the bed. Little did they realize, Ms. Nice was just
getting started. She had all intentions of feeling Malachi's
dick. She grabbed some tissue of the night stand and
cleaned Malachi off and took him in her mouth to bring
his member back to life. Malachi was definitely feeling
this chic and decided he definitely needed her information
so he could get back at her. Ms. Nice stood up and sat on
her knees about to kneel down on Malachi. Angel reached
on the ottoman at the end of the bed and grabbed a pack
of condoms and cleared her throat.

"No, no, remember our agreement." Angel said as she
handed the girl a condom. Malachi couldn't help but
laugh at Angel who was dead serious. Ms. Nice grabbed

the condom and rolled it down Malachi's dick with her mouth.

Shawty is a professional, Malachi thought as he laid back while Ms. Nice sat on him and rode him like a seasoned jockey. He was about to explode which obviously Ms. Nice was prepared for. She jumped off of him and took the condom off and licked up every bit of his juices like a straight up porn star. Angel was just looking and smiling – pleased with the outcome of her session. Malachi didn't have to figure out how he was going to get her information because when Angel turned to get her coat, she slipped him a little piece of paper and blew him a kiss. Yeah, he was definitely getting back at her, he thought and went to the bathroom for a second shower and to finally call it a night. Angel said she would be back and both women exited just a quietly as they had entered.

BABY G

Chapter 16

Malachi was trying his best to ignore his phone but it kept going off. He finally turned over after Angel kept complaining to see who it was. It was Levi, so he answered.

"Yo, why the fuck you not answering your phone?" Levi started soon as Malachi picked up.

"We been hit at the store. Get up and be on your way." Levi said and waited for a response. He knew Malachi was about to go off.

"What the fuck, what's missing? How much damage we talking about?"

Malachi was finally waking up. It seemed to him that he had just went to sleep after the private show Angel and her friend just gave him. His immediately started getting dressed all while still on the phone with Levi.

"Yo, let's just say all the clothes are still here and this shit is bad." Levi said walking back up to the store. Malachi was beyond furious. He was cursing at the air and getting dressed.

"Fuck, I will be there within the hour." Malachi said.

"Alright, I am walking into the store now. There are a few detectives here so I will take care of them and see you in a minute." Levi said before ending the call.

"What is wrong?" Angel said now fully awake.

"Shit, the store got jacked and it doesn't look good. Look, I will call and transfer enough money in your account so you can pay the movers and handle your business. Call me after you get settled and I will stop by."

"Alright, thanks." Angel said before turning back over, clearly with an attitude but Malachi brushed it off because he definitely didn't have time to worry about that.

Malachi was rushing and driving in and out of traffic trying to get to the store. This is when living so far was a turn off, when he needed to be back in the city within a moment's notice.

"Shit, Shit, Shit!" Malachi repeated as he hit his steering wheel.

That work and money if gone is going to cost them big. Thankfully, they would only have to worry about how it affected their own pockets since they made it a rule to always purchase their product up front. This business decision has proved to be the most valuable since at times like this, it could cost you your life with the kind of numbers they were playing with.

When Malachi arrived to the store, he was a little more calm but was anxious to hear what was missing. Thankfully all the police were gone so he walked in and started drilling the questions to Levi.

"Damn, hold up. I'm just as fucked up as you Malachi. Look, it's all gone. They got everything that was in the safe in the floor but didn't touch or know about the safe behind the clock." Levi went to explain that the detectives had all type of questions because a shoot-out was reported and blood was found on the scene.

"So, we know we have a wounded nigga involved."

"Man, that nigga gonna wish he was shot point blank that night." Malachi said pacing around the store. "So what did you tell the cops?"

"I took a few things off the racks and told them we didn't have a surveillance tape in the camera. Filled out a report and that was that, but one cop kept coming with suspicious questions so I know they have their doubts."

"Fuck them, they can't prove shit. Did you watch the tape yet?" Malachi questioned.

"Naw, they really just left so I was waiting for you to get here." Levi said as he popped the tape in and as both men got silent.

The robbers were extremely quick and didn't stay in the store more than eight minutes. It took a little time for them to get the safe open but they didn't have to look for anything which told them that someone had either seen them go in the safe or knew someone who did. Either way, they were determined to find out where their work was and more importantly revenge on the suckers who thought they could get away with it.

"They were extremely careful but check out the one dude there, he is walking with a slight limp." Malachi stated.

"Yo, good eye. I wouldn't have picked that up if you didn't notice it." Levi said and paused the tape. The two discussed whether they knew anyone with a limp and they couldn't come up with anyone.

"Well, we just need to keep our eyes and ears to the street. Don't tell no one about the robbery and see if anyone comes to us asking about it. It only put a little dent on our pockets so it is what it is." Malachi said calming himself down some. He was rubbing his forehead as he spoke.

"Yeah, somebody is bound to talk. So, what happened with Angel?" Levi asked.

"Shit, what time is it? Malachi looked at his Cartier watch and picked up the phone to dial his bank. He almost forgot about transferring the money to Angel's account. The mere mention of her name made him realize that he was really starting to despise their situation. He had to end this once and for all.

"Yo, you won't believe the shit she did last night." Malachi said to Levi while holding the phone to his ear.

"What she do?" Levi said shaking his head. Anticipating a story about her destroying the crib or something crazy like that.

"Yo, she had this bad chic come over and they performed a hell of a show for me. Girlfriend was Nice with a capital N." Malachi stated.

He put up his finger indicating he needed a second and gave the representative all of the information needed to transfer five thousand dollars in Angel's account.

When he got off, Levi couldn't wait to get the details. "So, who is the chick?" Levi asked.

"Angel called her Ms. Nice but home girl slipped me her number so I definitely will find out." Malachi stated with a grin.

"Yo, let's close up the store for the day and go hit the streets to see who's talking." Levi said while popping the tape out of the recorder and putting it in the safe behind the clock.

Yve was sitting in her living room smoking when the bell rang. She opened it and a disturbed Jayden walked in hyper than ever. Yve was immediately pissed off because once again he popped up without calling her.

"Why do you insist on popping up without calling?" Yve asked rolling her eyes at Jayden.

"Not now Yve, seriously." Jayden said while pacing the floor.

Yve paid him no mind and went back and grabbed her jay she was smoking. Jayden was cursing and fussing to himself and started making phone calls. Yve being high, resorted to ease dropping.

"What the hell happened last night? How the hell y'all get caught slipping?" Jayden screamed into the phone. Yve was about to tune him out when she saw he was discussing business until she heard him mention Hermano which was Levi's clothing label so she decided to listen more closely.

"Listen, I told y'all that Hermano shit was just a cover up. Them niggas going to be looking for their shit, believe that." Jayden said grabbing the hair from his beard.

"Y'all niggas just lay low until I get back with y'all. How that nigga Sweets doing? Tell that nigga he will live and keep it bandaged up. I will catch up with y'all later."

Jayden ended his call and walked over to the couch and sat beside Yve. Yve was now paranoid after smoking and hearing that conversation not knowing what the hell was going on. She was wondering if Jayden officially lost his mind and started following her and knew that she had been dealing with Levi, did he do something to him, she was a nervous wreck and it showed.

"What the hell is wrong with you?" Jayden asked and sat down on the sofa beside Yve.

"Nothing. Just high." Yve cursed herself at how dumb she sounded but that was the first thing that popped in her head.

"Let me hit that." Jayden said and took the jay from Yve. Yve was calming her nerves down because obviously Jayden didn't know her ties to Levi. She grabbed her phone and texted Layla nine, one, one.

Yve was thinking of a way to roll but she was sitting comfortably in her pajamas and had no idea how she was about to put Jayden out. Within minutes her cell phone was ringing with Layla on the phone.

"Yo, Chica – what's up?" Layla asked when Yve answered.

"Hey Girl, Ummm nothing. You want me to do what? Yve was trying to make it seem as if Layla needed her so she flipped the script.

"Huh? What the hell are you talking bout, Yve." Layla asked sounding irritated.

"Oh, okay. Well where are you?" Yve kept talking into the phone. Getting up to reiterate that the call was important.

"Girl, obviously you are tripping or can't really talk." Layla said laughing.

"Bingo!" Yve yelled.

"Oh, okay. I'm at home, why what's going on? Do you need me to come over there?" Layla asked concerned.

"Ummm, no – but I will be to you in about fifteen minutes." Yve said and disconnected the call before Layla could respond.

Jayden looked at Yve and saw the worry in her eyes.

"Yve, you okay? What's going on?" Jayden said and walked over to Yve.

"Everything is cool. Layla just needs me so I need to leave. Where were you headed to? I can catch up with you later 'cause I need to go get dressed and meet up with her." Yve said and started walking up the stairs with Jayden on her heels.

"Oh, well look – shit kind of hot at my spot right now so I need to lay low for a minute over here. I know you don't mind, right?" Jayden said waiting for an answer.

"Ummm, no – I guess that's fine. I should be back shortly." Yve said and hurried to get dressed.

Chapter 17

The whole drive to Layla's house Yve was contemplating calling Levi and discussing with him what she had heard since she had no idea what the real meaning behind it was. But something obviously bad happened and has Jayden stressed and from the sounds of it, someone even got hurt. Yve nerves were shot at this point so she smoked a jay not noticing it was making her even more paranoid. When she pulled up to Layla's house she hoped out and ran to the door and started ringing the doorbell like someone was chasing her.

"Damn, why the heck are you ringing the doorbell like you the damn Jehovah witnesses?" Layla asked and stood with her hands on her hip while Yve rushed by her.

"Girl, you are not going to believe what the hell I just heard." Yve said out of breath.

"Wait, I need some water, my mouth dry as shit." Yve said going further into the house and in the kitchen. Layla followed her anxious to hear what the heck was going on.

"Girl, spill it. Damn, the water – you need to tell me why you acting so damn hype. What happened?" Layla protested and waited for Yve to finish gulping down her water she had just poured into a glass from the automatic spout on the refrigerator.

"Okay, I was at home and here come Jayden ass popping up all nervous and shit. I was hitting a jay getting my relax on and I hear him talking on the phone and he had the nerve to mention *Hermano* which immediately got my attention so I listened a little more closely and heard him mention something about it being a cover-up and something about someone being hurt. Girl, I don't know what the hell happened but something went down. What do you think I should do?" Yve, finally stopped to take a breath.

"First, you need to relax 'cause it could be nothing, who is your loyalty with? Cause the way I see it, if you are feeling Levi like you say you are – then you need to call him and tell him what the hell you just heard." Layla said and pointed to the direction of the basement so they can go to her room.

"Layla, you know I am feeling Levi like shit but I am not certain what happened and I damn sure don't want him to think I'm involved in any kind of way since I am dealing with Jayden." Yve said and started pacing back and forth in Layla's room.

"Look Yve, the way I see it is that you have to let Levi know before he finds out anyway and then assumes you do have something to do with it. Look, call him and tell him to come over so you can talk to him." Layla said waiting for Yve to do just that. Layla decided to take this time to get dressed so she turned the CD player on and popped in Kelly Roland's new CD and immediately started jamming.

When Levi cell went off he noticed it was Yve, he started to forward it straight to voicemail but decided to just answer it and tell her he would get back at her after him and Malachi finished handling business but when he answered he heard the panic in her voice.

"Yo, what's going on Baby Girl? Are you okay?" Levi asked in a concerned voice.

"Ummm, yes and no. I really need to talk to you. Where are you?" Yve asked with a shaky voice.

"I'm riding around with Malachi. Right now we are Uptown. What happened?" Levi asked again.

"Okay, can you just come by Layla's house so I can speak with you? It's really important. I think I have some information that you might want to hear." Yve said trying to calm herself down.

"Oh, word. This wouldn't have anything to do with the fact my store just got robbed, would it?" Levi said with suspicion arising.

"Ummm, I had no idea your store got robbed but I'm sure it does have something to do with that. I just overheard something and think you might need to hear it." Yve said hesitantly.

"Alright, we on our way." Levi said and hung up before giving Yve a chance to say anything else.

Yve looked at Layla with worry in her eyes. Layla looked at Yve and knew her friend needed a hug so she did just that and embraced her. No more words were needed.

Layla continued getting dressed and sent Yve upstairs to grab a bottle of Moscato so they could unwind before Levi arrived.

Before either of them knew it, the doorbell was ringing. Yve looked at Layla and Layla told her to go open the door and bring him downstairs in her sitting area so they could talk.

Yve went upstairs and opened the door to both Levi and Malachi. She forgot to mention to Layla that he was with Levi but didn't think it would be a problem cause as far as she knew, they were getting along fine. Levi gave Yve a hug and kiss. He truly liked Yve and was beginning to think she was definitely the one for him. Malachi was a little impatient and was anxious to hear what Yve had to tell his brother. Yve escorted them to Layla's domain in her folk's basement. Layla came out of her room ready to greet Levi and stopped in her tracks when she saw Malachi.

"Hi Levi." Layla said. She cleared her throat and then softly said what's up to Malachi. Malachi knew she was still salty from him standing her up but he really didn't have time to entertain that right now.

"What's up, Layla. Look, you and I will handle our situation after we hear what Yve have to say. Can we please sit down and hear this now?" Malachi said letting his irritation show.

"Okay, have a seat." Yve said and sat down on the chaise in front of them. Layla stood beside her girl for moral support.

"Well, where do I start? Okay, here it is. Before you and I were dating," Yve started out looking directly into Levi's eyes to make sure she could see his reaction to her every word. "I was seeing this guy name Jayden and from time to time he still comes by to see me and well you know, we have been kicking for about a year now. And he popped up over my house this morning all hyped and I immediately gave him shade 'cause I definitely don't play that shit." Yve said and gave off an uneasy chuckle. She looked at Layla and then back at the guys. "Well, I was chilling and hitting a jay and didn't pay him any mind until he got on the phone and I heard him mention *Hermano* which immediately sparked my interest. I overheard him say something about y'all were going to be looking for y'all shit and that tell somebody name Sweets," she said snapping her fingers cause she couldn't remember the name earlier. "'To lay low,' and that was basically it." I had no idea about any of this Levi so I rushed out of there as soon as I could and came to talk to Layla who insisted I called you. So, here we are."

"Word? So Jayden and some dude name Sweets got our shit." Malachi said, punching his fist into his palm. Layla decided not to open her mouth about knowing someone name Sweets because one she wasn't sure if it was the same person and two, she didn't want to get involved in this mess since she did grow up with Sweets.

"Damn Baby," Levi said and grabbed Yve. He gave her a long kiss and was so happy she trusted him enough to tell him what she heard. "Yo, I know this was hard for you but word, I knew there was a reason I was falling for your ass. You thorough as shit." Levi said and embraced Yve.

"Damn, later for all that lovey-dovey shit. But, on the real – thanks Yve for the info." Malachi said as well.

"So, Yve, where can we find this cat at?" Malachi asked. Yve knew the question was coming and she really didn't know how Levi would react to this.

"Well, he is at my house. He asked if he could lay low there this morning so I am scared shitless and don't want this drama." Yve said and looked at Levi.

"Baby, you have nothing to worry about. When this is all said and done, I will buy you another house if need be. We got this. Give Malachi and I some time to work out a plan but just stay away today and tell him you will be home around eleven o'clock. I promise, nothing will happen to your place and I will make sure there are no traces back to you. Let me get your key."

Yve knew he was talking about possibly killing Jayden and she didn't know how she felt about this. She looked at Layla as she was taking her key off the key ring.

"Look y'all, this is some real gangsta stuff, so just don't give out any more details 'cause the less we know, the better." Layla said and gave Yve a smile and a look to tell her everything will be alright.

Malachi looked at Layla and was impressed with her whole demeanor but definitely not surprised. The girl was definitely ride or die and he knew she had it in her to hold a nigga down from the first day he met her.

"Layla, can I speak to you privately for a minute?" Malachi asked.

Layla rolled her eyes and led him to her bedroom. When they got in there he closed the door and began speaking.

"Look, you already know I am feeling you like shit." Layla looked at him and rolled her eyes ready to jump down his throat but he put up his finger silencing her.

"The other day I was handling business so I had to cancel plans with you but I swear you were on my mind the entire night."

He really believed what he was saying. Even though he was with Angel and Ms. Nice, he was wishing he was with Layla.

"Look, I'm not tripping. Apparently you had better things to do so it is what it is." Layla responded not sounding convincing.

She was ready to walk out the room but Malachi grabbed her and kissed her. She didn't resist even though her heart was telling her to. Malachi was the first to pull back and he looked directly in her eyes.

"Look, we need to go handle business but let Yve stay here with you tonight and we will call y'all once we know everything is okay."

Layla nodded and escorted Malachi out of her room.

To get Yve's mind off things, Layla called Monique so the girls could go shopping for the all-white party which was the upcoming weekend. After all the much hype, the girls were not going to miss this party which was sure to bring out the best of the best.

As the girls were walking out, Nate and Monique were pulling up. He stepped out of his truck and walked up to Layla with a box in his hand. Both Monique and Yve were all up in their business.

Layla looked at them, cleared her throat and rolled her eyes at them letting them know they were being nosey. Not as if they cared because they kept standing right there on the front lawn of Layla's folks crib. All Layla could think about is she is so glad Levi and Malachi had not been there when Nate pulled up.

Nate came face to face to Layla and kissed her. She looked at him and felt his forehead.

"Uhhh, are you okay? You know you been acting a little strange these last couple of days, right?" Layla said backing up a little. Nate pushed the box in her hand and told her to open it.

"What is it?" Layla asked smiling from ear to ear.

"Open it and find out." He said with this cockiness that turned Layla on. She did as she was told and opened the box. She was stunned. It was a platinum necklace that read, *Baby G*. The *G* was in gold which made it stand out and diamonds were encrusted throughout each letter. To say the least, it was hot.

"Oh my goodness. Nate, it's beautiful." Layla said with her mouth still open.

"Not as beautiful as you. Layla, we need to have a serious talk so after the party tomorrow, you are coming with me for the weekend. With you moving into your new place and all, I want to make sure we straighten out some things." Nate said and gave her a big kiss and a hug as he stepped off saying his goodbyes.

"What does it say?" Yve and Monique asked in unison.

Layla both showed the girls her gift proudly. The girls awed over the beautiful piece of jewelry.

"Now you know that is hot, right? Shit, look like Nate got more money than we think." Monique said and the girls all looked at each other giggling.

"Yeah, Chica. I love it. It really symbolizes what you mean to him. I think in his own way he is letting you know that you are definitely his." Yve said while admiring the necklace leaving Layla to ponder on what she just said.

"Alright y'all. Let's go to the mall. I want to find a really cute dress for the all-white party." Monique said as they got in the car.

BABY G

Chapter 18

Malachi and Levi were on the phone calling some of their peeps. They only trusted a handful of dudes in the area so for the job they needed done, they called their goons from New York to make the ride down. That gave them the next four hours to put their plan together and another three to execute it. Malachi was more ruthless out of the two but Levi definitely was no push over. The guys decided to split up and get the items they needed off their list. It was all normal supplies that anyone that planned on killing someone would need. The mask, the rope, the plastic, the weapons, and the list went on.

Meanwhile, the girls headed to Georgetown to find their outfits for the party. On the ride there, they caught Monique up on what Yve had heard and what may go down later that night. Monique couldn't believe what she was hearing and kept saying she had a bad feeling about all of it and didn't know if she really trusted Malachi and Levi. Yve was getting tired of talking about it and changed the subject. Instead they discussed the type of outfits they were all looking for the remainder of the ride there.

When they arrived in Georgetown they went in every store imaginable. They spent hours shopping, each girl finding a very different look for the all-white party. Layla found a very sexy white corset which complimented her DD cup breast with a cute white fitted skirt, Monique found a sexy white fitted dress that was trimmed in black and equally complimented her assets, while Yve found some cute white shorts and a white sheer blouse that hung off her shoulders detailed with silver ruffle trim around the edges. To say the least, the girls were very pleased with their outfits and decided it was time to get something to eat. The girls decided on the waterfront restaurant *Tony & Joe's* since it was still kind of nice outside. They all ordered wine and searched the seafood menu for their meal.

"Yve, are you okay?" Monique asked noticing that Yve wasn't talking much.

"Yeah, I guess. I really don't want any of this to come back at me and for Jayden to find out I told Levi what I heard."

"Well, I'm sure that Levi and Malachi are about their word and will make sure you're good. Just think, you can stay with me and help me move into my new place." Layla said.

"Oh, shoot, that's right Layla. With everything going on, I forgot you're ready to move." Yve said snapping out of her trance.

"Yes, so y'all just be ready early so we can handle our business. The beauty is that all we have to move are clothes since the furniture and all will be delivered. All I need for y'all to do is help me set up the kitchen, the bathroom, and help me make the place look like a home." Layla said all smiles.

"Girl, you know that's my cup of tea so you are in good hands." Monique said giving Layla a high five.

The girls drinks came and they ordered their food. They sat around talking and mostly about the all-white party and loving the fact that the area's hottest band was performing along with Jill Scott.

"Yes, this is going to be a hot party ladies." Layla said raising her glass followed by the Yve and Monique.

When the girl's bill came, they decided to divide it by three and each added an extra four dollars for the tip. They were satisfied and decided it was time to roll out.

Back in the car, Yve started rolling a jay because her nerves were still on edge. She was determined not to worry. Her phone pulled her out of her thoughts. It was Levi.

"Hey Babe, what's up?" Yve answered.

"Yo, it's getting late Babe – remember under no circumstances are you to go home tonight. Call that nigga and tell him you will be home around eleven o'clock." Levi instructed and told Yve he loved her which was a shock to her but really nice to hear.

"Okay, Baby – I got you and I love you too." Yve responded feeling like everything would be just fine.

At times like this, Yve wished her grandmother was still living in the area and not all the way in Charlotte.

"You love who?" Layla yelled looking back at Yve grabbing her attention.

"You are so nosey, Layla. If you must know, that was Levi, and yes – I guess I am falling in love with him. What's not to love? The nigga is thorough as hell and treats me better than any man I have ever been with. And it's not even about the money or nothing like that. He just has an aura about him that makes me feel loved, respected, and safe." Yve said smiling.

"Well, shit. Ain't nothing wrong with that. That's how Nate makes me feel." Layla said. "But he just doesn't know he's about to let someone else slip easily in that space."

The girls hit the jay and headed back to Layla's house.

"How about we have a girl's night since this will be the last time we all get together like this over my folks house." Layla exclaimed.

"Well, I kind of have a date with Carlos tonight." Monique said not wanting to be the party pooper. "I guess I can change our plans though to another night."

"Cool, well it's settled. Stop at the liquor store so we can get a couple bottles of wine." Layla said passing the jay to Monique.

"Naw, I'm good. Let me see my phone so I can call Carlos." Monique said pointing at her purse.

They pulled up to the liquor store and Layla got out since Monique was still on the phone talking to Carlos and she knew Yve wasn't going to get out and go in.

When they arrived back at Layla's house, they sat in the car spraying a little freshener hoping to rid themselves of the smell of the weed that they were sure got into their clothes. Layla mom was sitting on the couch. They all spoke to Layla's mom and tried to hurry down the basement.

"Layla, come here." Her mom yelled from their living room.

"Yes, Mommy?" Layla responded sounding irritated.

"Layla, have you all been smoking? 'Cause y'all stink with all that whatever stinky stuff y'all call yourselves spraying." Layla's mom asked looking at her daughter's glossy eyes.

"Mom, why do you ask me questions to things you already know the answer to?" Layla asked back rolling her eyes.

"Excuse me? I will ask whatever the hell I want to and if you know what I know, you would want to be getting yourself together. Running around here smoking all the time and doing whatever you want like you some hood trash. I raised you better than this and you need to get yourself right with God." Layla's mother preached.

Layla always knew it was just a matter of seconds when her mom was talking to her before her she started bringing God in on their conversations.

"Mommy, I am not out her just wilding out. I will get a good job and make you proud. I'm just having a little fun and I'm definitely not out here harming anyone so can you please lay off a bit?" Layla requested hoping she was getting her point across to her mother.

"Okay, will suit yourself Layla. You know my doors will always be open if you feel like you ever need to come back. I know how hard it is being independent but I guess you just have to see for yourself. Y'all girls have a good night and you better make sure you'll still be in church every Sunday."

Layla couldn't believe her mom picked this very moment to have a heart-to-heart with her. But, she loved her mom and knew it was some truth to what she was saying to her. She was grateful to have the kind of parents she had. She gave her mother a kiss, grabbed three glasses out of the kitchen and headed down the basement to hang out with the girls.

Yve and Monique were already undressed and in their night clothes so Layla handed them the glasses and followed suit getting undressed and slipping on a pair of boxers and a tank top. Yve looked at the clock and realized she never called Jayden to tell him what time she would be there as Levi instructed but she wasn't too late so she excused herself from the girls and made the call. He answered on the first ring.

"Damn, I've been calling you all day. When you coming home?" He asked.

"Ummm, well – my battery was dead but I should be home by eleven o'clock." Yve responded having to think quickly.

"Alright, stop and bring me something to eat when you come." Jayden said and they said their goodbyes.

It was ten o'clock and Yve nerves were shot. She went back in the room with the girls, picked up her glass Layla poured and downed it in one gulp.

"Okay, I see you on edge." Layla said refilling Yve's glass.

The girls sat around and caught up on each other's lives. Monique let the girls know that she was really feeling Carlos and that they had been speaking on making it more permanent and considering moving in together. She was a little down about her mom's condition and possibly having to give up her apartment. So, Monique was a little uneasy for that reason. The girls understood where she was coming from but Layla also voiced that her mom had been away for a couple of years now with no signs of getting better so she should do what makes her happy. Monique appreciated hearing the truth from her girlfriends and loved these little girls nights out they shared.

Malachi and Levi were at one of their dope boys cribs uptown with their goons from New York going over the final details before they make their move. The plan was to move in on Jayden unexpectedly and swiftly. They were not to kill him in Yve's crib and were not to leave any traces of him that would be lead back to Yve. Levi made sure they all knew the importance of getting him out of Yve's crib and taking him to their warehouse on Ritchie Marlboro Road to get the details they needed from him. They wanted their work and cash back and they wanted it back that night.

Malachi and Levi had gotten a U-Haul truck from a dope fiend earlier that day so they drove that and their goons followed in their ride. Malachi had a Desert Eagle and Levi was polishing his Glock. Needless to say, the brothers were ready.

They pulled up to Yve's house and parked the U-Haul in the back alley of her house. Thankfully it wasn't a neighborhood were dudes were hanging out all times of the night. So, for the most part, no one was really out. Malachi stayed around the back of the house with two of the New Yorkers and Levi went around through the front with the other two. He slowly and quietly put the key in the door unlocking it and opening it slowly. He had only really been to Yve's house maybe twice and the first time he hadn't come in. So, he was only a little familiar with his surroundings as they walked in. He noticed all the lights were off downstairs which was a good sign cause that meant the bamma was upstairs and relaxing.

He walked to the back of her house past the kitchen and unlocked the back door to let Malachi and the other two guys in. Levi signaled to them that Jayden was upstairs. So, they slowly crept up the steps all with mask on. Two of the goons stayed downstairs by the steps with their weapons drawn. It was truly a scene out of a movie. Yve's door was a little down the hall and was open only slightly. They could hear the television on and it appeared that he was watching a flick. They signaled on three to one another to go in.

"Raise up, Nigga." Malachi spoke with authority. Jayden was truly caught off guard with his member in hand. He was definitely not expecting this since he was about to bust any minute.

"What the fuck?" Is all he could say before Malachi reached down and hit him with his Dessert Eagle and snatched him up. Levi and the other goons had their guns drawn on him and escorted him down the stairs with him pleading that he had money and whatever else they wanted on him if they would give him a chance to get it.

"Nigga, that's the least of our worries. We want what's ours so shut the fuck up and move." Levi said pointing towards the remaining stairs.

Their boys that were at the bottom of the stairs grabbed a hold of him and started tying the rope around his hands.

"Hold up, pull up your damn pants." Levi said – "I know you didn't think you would feel my woman's pussy ever again?" Levi Chuckled.

All kind of thoughts were running through Jayden's head but one thing for sure, if he got out of this alive, Yve was dead. He did as he was instructed and tried to play cool but deep down, he knew all of his past sins had just caught up with him.

BABY G

Chapter 19

The guys pulled up to the warehouse with Levi jumping out first to open the garage door. He opened it and Malachi drove the U-Haul in followed by the boys from New York in their ride. Levi quickly closed the garage door. Levi and Malachi had owned the abandoned warehouse building for several years and just hadn't thought about what they wanted to do with it but as luck would have it, it worked out perfect for this occasion. They all walked to the back of the U-Haul and swung the door open to find Jayden with this hard look on his face and no fear in sight. His hands were tied behind his back and he immediately started asking questions for days.

"What the fuck is all this about? Man pussy ain't never been worth all of this." Jayden said with a sinister grin.

Levi walked up to him and stole him right in his jaw. "Nigga this ain't got shit to do with no motha-fuckin' pussy. Bitch, this here is about our dough and work you stole from us." Levi was in the zone and was very animated while he talked.

Jayden looked at the two niggas standing in front of him and immediately put two and two together to identify them as the infamous *Hermano* owners. He was fucked and all he could do was looked stunned.

"Oh, you ain't got shit to say now, huh?" Malachi said getting angrier by the second. He instructed his boys to move him to the middle of the floor and tie him up to the chair he sat in the open area. The warehouse was very cold and dark with cement floors and only four windows at the very top near the ceilings. It was empty besides a few knick-knack stuff like clothing rods and steel wardrobes scattered about. Malachi walked over to where Jayden was seated now and saw a little more fear in his eyes then before.

"Yo, I'm only going to ask you this one damn time. If I don't like the answer, I promise you that a long slow painful death awaits you." Malachi said while only inches away from Jayden's face.

"Man, I don't..." Is all Jayden could say before Malachi pistol came crashing down on his nose surely breaking it. Jayden winced out in pain and shook his head several times. His hands were now tied behind his back.

"Nigga, we doing the talking until you asked to speak, don't say shit." Levi chimed in. Their goons standing around all started chuckling and were just waiting for the command to dead Jayden.

"You only have one time to respond and I better like the answer. Where the fuck is our money at nigga?" Malachi said not taking his eyes off Jayden.

"Look, I don't know where your shit is. We never made off with your shit." Jayden spoke.

"What the fuck you mean? Our shit is gone so you playing games – huh? You obviously think this shit a game." Malachi said and reached for his boy pistol with the silencer on it and shot Jayden in his right foot. Jaden screamed but unfortunately for him, there wasn't anyone out in that area at that time of night. Not to mention, the thickness of the walls were sure to keep his screams from being heard.

"Yo, one more time. Where the fuck is our money and work at?" Malachi was losing patience with Jayden and was ready to give the command.

"Listen," Jayden pled.

"I swear we don't have your shit. We got jacked when coming out of your store." Jayden spoke in between sobs. "Apparently someone knew what was up and took the shit from us when we were coming out. We had a shootout and all coming out from there. Look, I got paper so this was just some shit one of my boys conjured up and I went along with it. If you let me go…"

Levi was tired of hearing this nigga talk. "Yo, shut the fuck up." Levi commanded. He looked at Malachi and no words were needed because it was obvious no more information was going to come out of him. He seemed to possibly be telling the truth but the fact remained that they had enough balls to come rob them.

"Yo, who the fuck else was with you?" Malachi turned around and asked.

"Man, look if y'all going to kill me, go ahead but I'm not about to snitch on no damn body. So, do what you must." Jayden said. Obviously coming to terms that his time on earth was drawing near. He was going out like a soldier in his eyes.

"Alright, if that's the way you want it." Malachi looked at the goons and gave them instructions to dead the nigga and drop him over the Delaware Memorial Bridge on their way home. It was a done deal. Malachi and Levi pulled the goons to the side, gave them a package containing money, instructions to burn the U-Haul, and prepared to leave.

"Fuck you niggas." Is all that could be heard before one of the goons put a bullet in the center of Jayden's forehead. Malachi and Levi left out the side door and jumped in Levi's BMW and sped off.

"Seriously, I am exhausted." Layla said looking around her new condo. She was extremely pleased with how fast they moved her in with the help of her parents and how everything just fell into place. It was now only Yve, Monique, and Layla sitting in the beautiful condo gathering up all the trash. It was three o'clock in the afternoon and all day Yve's mind had been drifting off to the other night. She had still not been back home too fearful of what she would find. Levi told her everything was good and she could return the next day but Yve was not trying to hear that.

"Yo, so what time are we meeting up to get dressed for tonight?" Layla asked interrupting Yve's thoughts and getting Monique's attention from in the kitchen. Tonight was finally the night of the all-white party. With so much going on, the girls felt as if they needed a really nice night out.

"Well, I plan to meet y'all there because Carlos is taking me to see *Mike Brooks* tonight at the Comedy Club prior to going to the party. Matter of fact, I really need to be going home so I can get a little rest and get dressed." Monique said grabbing her purse and keys and giving both of the girls a hug. "Layla, honey – we pulled off this pink and it looks absolutely gorgeous." Monique complimented as she walked to the door.

"Yes, thanks to you for helping me pick out all of the accessories. I really am pleased. Thanks boo and we will see you tonight." Layla said getting up to lock the door behind Monique.

Layla turned around and looked at Yve. "So, Chica – it's time we head over to your place. Are you ready?" Layla asked looking at Yve.

"Sure, let me roll one and get my nerves right." Yve said as she pulled out a zip lock bag and a blunt and started rolling her peace of mind.

"Alright, Girl. But you are not smoking that up in here. I do not want my furniture already smelling like no damn weed so let's hit that in your car." Layla said walking to get her purse and Yve's keys from out of her room.

When they arrived at Yve's house, they both were visibly nervous and didn't know what to expect. Yve unlocked the door and walked in followed by Layla.

"Don't shut the door just in case we have to run our happy asses outta here." Yve said to Layla.

The girls walked around the first level of Yve's home looking to see if anything was out of place. So far everything seemed to be in place. Yve kept imagining what that night might have been like for Jayden thinking that it was her coming in the house but being snatched up by a bunch of unknown fellas. Her heart went out to him and she knew that the inevitable had happened that night considering she hadn't heard from him at all. But the truth of the matter was that she was not in love with Jayden nor did she tell him to rob anyone is how she reasoned that her actions were justified. Levi was going to meet her at the all-white party later that night and it would be the first time they seen each other since the day she handed him her key.

Yve was first to walk up the stairs. She moved slow and deliberately as if she was trying not to wake someone. Layla followed Yve nudging her to walk up. Yve turned around and gave Layla a scowl.

"Look, scary cat, let me go in front of you." Layla said moving around Yve and walking up the steps.

Layla checked Yve's office and guest bedroom and nothing was out of place. They both stood looking at Yve's door which was wide open. Yve walked in first and to her surprise, nothing was out of place. In fact, the room was beautiful and decorated with a new comforter set and accessories and rose pedals were sprawled across her bed in a heart shape. She was definitely taken back. She grabbed the note in the center of the roses.

"Yve,

You have truly showed me how much you are down for a nigga like me and I just wanted to put a smile on that beautiful face.

Levi

Yve was shocked and at the moment, she felt that she definitely made the right decision by telling Levi what she had overheard.

"Girl, look at your bathroom. Boyfriend went all out." Layla said looking at the matching accessories in the bathroom and the rose pedals all over her floor and candles lined around her tub.

"Yes, he did. I love it." Yve said twirling around admiring Levi's thoughtfulness.

"Glad he had enough sense not to light the candles." Layla giggled.

"Girl, go downstairs and close the front door while I call Levi and grab a bag of my things." Yve called Levi and told him she loved what he did to her room and bathroom and thanked him for making her feel at ease. He of course said it was only something small and that he couldn't wait to see her that night at the party. They said their goodbyes and disconnected.

Layla came back up the stairs with a bottle of water for her and Yve and plopped down on Yve's bed while Yve was gathering up her under clothes and accessories for tonight.

Yve stopped packing and looked at Layla.

"You know what, how about you take my car, go ahead and go home since you hadn't had a chance to enjoy your new place alone and I will get Levi to come pick me up. I miss my house and just want to soak in the tub for a while." Yve said sounding a little giddy. She truly was happy to be home and wanted to enjoy the ambience that Levi took the time to set up for her.

"Okay, honey. If you really feel like you are okay – that works for me." Layla said grabbing her Gucci shades off the bed and matching satchel from the floor by the foot of Yve's bed.

"Yeah, thankfully Levi kept his word and left no reminder of you-know-who." Yve said referring to Jayden. "So, I feel comfortable. I'm going to call Nana and see how the real South is treating her and relax before tonight. We should get there around eleven o'clock." Yve said walking Layla downstairs.

She handed Layla her keys and locked the door behind her. As soon as Yve locked the door she felt an eerie feeling creep up on her and she started to change her mind and call Layla back but quickly dismissed the feeling and headed back upstairs. She grabbed the cordless phone from her nightstand and dialed her grandmother's phone number. It took her a little while before finally getting an answer.

"Hi Nana." Yve said so happy to talk to her grandmother.

"Hi Baby," Yve's grandmother replied.

Yve caught her grandmother up on all of her current projects and even told her about Levi. She of course didn't mention anything concerning the Jayden situation and definitely didn't want to worry her grandmother. Yve kept the phone to her shoulder and went in the bathroom to run her bath water.

"So, Baby – when do you plan to come visit me?" Yve's grandmother asked her.

"Very soon Nana. As a matter of fact, the CIAA is right around the corner so me and the girls will come stay with you that weekend." Yve said and explained to her grandmother what the CIAA event was.

Her grandmother told her she couldn't wait to see them. Yve was caught between listening to her grandmother and trying to see whether she heard something downstairs. She thought she had heard some sort of clinking sound but between the water, her grandmother, and her moving around in her room – she dismissed it and continued with her conversation.

"Well Nana, I am going to jump in the tub and talk to you later. Yes, I love you too." Yve said hanging up and turning the bath water off. She then turned around and immediately dropped the phone and stood eye to eye looking down the barrel of a gun.

BABY G

Chapter 20

Layla arrived back at her condo and walked in feeling refreshed. It was now eight o'clock and already dark outside.

"Where did the day go." Layla said to the walls in her condo.

Since Yve informed her that her and Levi would arrive by eleven o'clock, she had plenty of time to relax she thought until her cell phone started going off.

"Yeah?" she answered. She was feeling a little annoyed since she was visibly tired.

"Yeah? Is that how you answer the phone Baby G?"

Layla was actually very pleased to hear Nate's voice on the other end of her line. "Hey Hun, what's going on? I know y'all coming to the all-white party, right?" Layla asked taking off her shoes and laying stomach down on her bed.

"Yeah, we're coming through. You remember what I told you, right?" Nate asked.

"No, what?" Layla asked not having a clue as to what Nate was talking about.

"I told you I want you to come with me after the party so we can spend some time together and I need to speak with you about something important." He snapped. Obviously he was feeling some kind of way that Layla had forgotten that he just laced her neck and told her he wanted to talk to her. He was prepared to finally make her his. He had been planning to originally take her away on a trip but he had just opened a detail shop with his new ends and didn't want to leave until everything was fully up and running worry free.

"Oh, my bad Nate. So much has been going on that I totally forgot. But, I got you. I am all yours after the party." Layla stated matter of fact.

"Cool, big head. See you later." Nate laughed and the phone line went dead.

Layla put her phone down and went in her bathroom to run a steamy hot bath. Soon as she turned the water on she heard her phone ringing again. *Damn, what now?* she thought.

"Dang, hello?" Layla said with an attitude answering her phone without bothering to look at the caller ID.

"Damn, what's up with you Sexy?" Malachi responded sounding sexy and cool all at the same time.

"Oh, my bad Malachi. I have just been trying to relax and just can't seem to do that before I have to be out of here." Layla explained while gathering up her Strawberries & Champagne body wash and lighting her tub candles that were set up neatly on the ledge of her soak in tub.

"Oh, word. You going to that party tonight, yo?" Malachi asked already knowing that they were according to his brother.

"Yeah, we're going. I am about to jump in the tub now." Layla said feeling some kind of way about Malachi.

"Damn, that's a nice visual Ma." Malachi said matching her tone.

Layla just giggled.

"So, how are you liking your new place?" Malachi asked.

Layla was surprised he remembered that she moved with everything that's been going on lately.

"Oh, I love it." Layla sang as she walked in the bathroom to cut her water off. "It has a peace in here that I can't seem to explain." Layla said but in actuality, she could explain it.

Her parents anointed every room in her new condo and prayed before they left. They had all the girls in tears when it was all said and done. Layla feeling like she was tired of the same ole, same ole. Yve was thinking about her grandmother and Jayden, and Monique just thankful for her Mom and Carlos.

"Yo, well I'm trying to see you after the party tonight." Malachi said snapping Layla out of her thoughts from earlier that day.

"Ummm, well tonight might not be good. But we can play it by ear." Layla said not wanting to brush Malachi off completely.

"Alright shorty, that's cool. I'm telling you that there's no need to keep running 'cause I will get you sooner or later." Malachi said with a cockiness and chuckle.

"Yeah, yeah – heard it all before." Layla sang and busted out laughing. "I will see you later tonight."

The two ended their phone conversation and Layla walked over to her CD player and popped in Beyoncé. She turned to the fourth single, *Best thing I Never Had* and headed to her bathroom and relaxed in her tub.

In Laurel, Monique and Carlos were enjoying dinner and getting ready for their show to start at the *Comedy Club*. When the waitress came back and asked if they were okay, they both ordered another drink and thanked her.

"If I didn't tell you yet, you look beautiful in that white." Carlos complimented.

"Actually, that is the third time you told me and you know you are also looking quite dapper as well." Monique said leaning over to give Carlos a kiss.

They were sitting side by side and enjoying every minute of each other. Monique couldn't believe her luck. Not too long ago she was single and loving every moment of it but in no time at all, Carlos came and erased all memories of her ever enjoying anything else but being with him. She looked over at him and smiled. The Club owner got on stage and welcomed everyone out and told them they were in for a great show. Everyone started clapping and whistling and *Mike Brooks* came running out on the stage. He wasted no time getting right into it. He started off with some light jokes talking about the audience and in no time, he had everybody about to fall out of their seats. To say the least, Monique was really enjoying herself until she suddenly felt an eerie feeling wash over her. She immediately thought of Yve. She turned her attention away from Carlos and the funny man on stage and texted both Layla and Yve to ask whether everything was okay. Carlos noticed Monique was somewhere else and asked her if everything was okay. She nodded and got back into the show. A few minutes later Layla was responding and letting her know everything was fine and that they would meet at the club shortly. She felt more at ease and didn't trip off of Yve not responding since she figured her and Layla were still together.

Layla arrived at the all-white party and was not surprised to see how the promoters pulled out all stops to make this event a success. Sky lights were able to be seen from miles away and the entrance to the club looked more like a movie premier with red carpet and cameras flashing from every angle. Layla checked her face to make sure if any of the pictures were going to be posted on Facebook, she would be sure to look her best. She realized everybody looked at everybody else's profiles and that there is always a hater or two lurking and waiting for you to be off your game. Well, tonight they were out of luck because Layla was flawless in her white corset and tight mini skirt. Her make-up was on point and her hairstylist had made sure her thick long hair was full of bouncy flowing curls and since Layla had it pin curled all day, it was not a strand out of place.

Layla walked in like she owned the club. She immediately headed straight to the bar and ordered a *Peach Ciroc* and pineapple. She had heard so much about the new peach flavor that Diddy been promoting that she had to try it for herself.

"Damn, this good." Layla said aloud after taking her first sip.

Layla checked her watch and decided she had better call Yve because she didn't know where their table was supposed to be. Before she could pull out her phone, Layla was greeted by Lyn and Nut. Lyn was looking just as beautiful in a white fitted mini and black stilettos and accessories. She gave Layla a hug, followed by Nut.

"Hey Layla, where is Nate?" Nut asked looking around the packed club.

"Oh, I'm not sure. I just arrived about ten minutes ago. This was my first stop." Layla said gesturing at her glass.

"Where is Yve and Monique?" Lyn asked.

"Oh, they should be here any minute." Layla said looking at her Cartier watch.

The girls chatted a bit while Nut ordered a bottle for him and Lyn. He offered Layla a glass but she declined and decided to stick with her Ciroc Peach and pineapple drink until they finally got to their tables.

"Hey Girl!" Monique yelled coming up to Layla from behind.

"Hey Honey." Layla greeted her and Carlos both with hugs. Monique looked around before asking about Yve.

"Girl, I'm not sure where her and Levi are. She told me she was going to meet us up here and ride with him." Layla said looking around.

Before either could say anything else. Levi and Malachi were making their way over to the bar but not before getting stopped by every female and male in the club. Layla watched them closely and couldn't help but admire Malachi's presence whenever he walked in a room.

He looks damn good too in his all-white, Layla thought licking her lips.

"Damn, you're looking sexy." Malachi said, walking up to Layla and taking her out of her naughty thoughts.

"Ummm, hi Malachi." Layla blushed.

"Baby G." Malachi said admiring Layla's iced out necklace.

"Oh" Layla said forgetting she wore her necklace. "It was a gift from a friend." Layla smiled nervously.

She looked past Malachi as Levi was walking up and noticed Yve was not in eye sight.

"Levi, where is my girl?" Layla asked.

"Huh, I was about to ask you the same thing. I thought the two of you were coming together." Levi asked looking at Layla.

They were shouting trying to talk over the music and caught Monique's attention.

"So, she is not with you?" Monique questioned Levi.

"I left her at home and she said she was going to catch a ride with you." Layla said pulling out her phone to call Yve.

Everybody sat waiting for Layla's conversation to begin with Yve. Layla was visible shaken up a bit. She hadn't heard from Yve since she left her house hours ago. The phone was on its fourth ring and Yve's voicemail picked up.

"Damn, I'm not getting an answer." Layla said.

She looked at Monique and before either of them could say a word, Nate and Al walked up to where they all were standing.

Nate had a mug on his face, obviously not happy to see Malachi and Levi standing there.

"What's good?" Nate said looking at Layla.

"Hi Nate." Layla greeted him with a hug and introduced everyone. Neither Nate nor Malachi shook hands but that was the least of Layla's worries.

"Yve is missing." Layla said to Nate.

"What you mean, she missing?" Nate asked.

Layla broke down the whole story about how they went to her house earlier and how Yve had a change of heart and wanted to ride with Levi so in turn, Layla left her thinking Yve would be okay. While Layla was explaining to Nate and Al, Levi was standing to the side calling Yve's phone. Someone answered the phone on the first ring.

"Just the nigga I was hoping would call."

Levi felt his blood start to boil and he checked to look at the screen on his phone. He wanted to make sure he dialed the right number.

"Man, who the fuck is this?" Levi shouted.

"Yo, while you out partying it up. I got your Bitch." The unknown caller on the other end said before disconnecting the call.

"Yo, that was somebody that answered Yve's phone. This shit is not good. Somebody got her." Levi said to no one in particular while looking at the entire group.

"What?" Layla responded while losing her balance.

Monique grabbed her friend's arm and they all headed outside of the club.

"What the fuck is going on?" Nate asked aloud. "Who would want to kidnap Yve?"

Monique started from the beginning explaining to Nate and Al, how Yve overhead Jayden discussing the store robbery and that she put Levi on point. Nate and Al didn't let on that they knew about the store robbery and possibly was also to blame for what was taking place.

"Damn, so do you guys know who has anything to do with this?" Nate said looking directly at Malachi. Malachi picked up on the accusatory tone in Nate's voice and matched his glare eye on.

"Naw, if we did – the motherfucker's family would already be making funeral arrangements." Malachi said looking straight in Nate's eyes.

"Look, standing here talking about the..." Was all Layla could say before Levi cell phone started ringing. He looked up at everybody after checking the caller ID. "This is the nigga again."

"Well find out where he has her." Layla said looking at Levi.

"Yo, Nigga!" Was all Levi could get out before the caller on the other end demanded his attention.

"Yo, listen here, I'm holding these cards so play your part and shut the fuck up." He demanded. "This pretty thing right here is just fine," he said looking over at Yve crying with tape on her mouth and make-up running down her face. "This is how this is going to work – you can have your bitch back in exchange for Jayden or three hundred thousand cash money. And since I know you already smashed off my homey, make sure all the bread is there. See you tomorrow night at nine sharp in front of the Warner Theatre and don't even try anything stupid cause there will be a packed house tomorrow."

The line went dead and Levi was left standing there looking at the phone.

"What did he say? Is Yve okay?" Layla was throwing questions at Levi.

He looked at everybody and spoke. "The nigga wants three hundred thousand by tomorrow night and wants us to meet him at the Warner Theatre."

"What the hell? Why would he think someone has that type of money?" Layla said looking at Malachi and Levi.

"Yo, Shawty – the money is not an issue." Malachi spoke up first. "But who is to say he will give Yve back once he gets the money? We need to think like an average nigga in the street would and play this thing out."

Nate was contemplating what Malachi was saying and acknowledging to himself that he did have a part in this, he felt obligated to help not to mention Yve was his homegirl too. He knew that it would break Layla's heart if something happened to her.

"Look, I'm not sure what kind of pull y'all got out here and what y'all can do in such short time, but me and my mans definitely can assist with this situation. Yve is our homegirl too." Nate spoke up, looking at Al.

"For sure, we definitely down." Al said agreeing with Nate.

"Yo, I'm not in the streets like that no more but I damn sure can help. I don't want my baby losing any unnecessary sleep either." Carlos said grabbing Monique's hand a little tighter.

From the outside looking in, the nine of them huddled up in their all white looked like a scene out of a gangster movie.

"Okay, it's all settled. Let's get my baby back." Levi said and walked towards Valet to give the attendant the ticket for his car.

BABY G

Chapter 21

Yve sat with her back against a cement wall and on a cold floor. She was stripped down to her under garments for no other purpose than humiliation and tied up against her will. So far the kidnapper had yet to get aggressive with her because she cooperated from the time she was introduced to the eye of the gun. She heard the conversation that the guy had with Levi and only hoped he would spare that money for her life. She knew that they hadn't been together long but she felt a connection with him that she hadn't with any other man in her life. She just prayed he felt it enough to have sympathy and rescue her.

She couldn't help but to think about how none of this would be going on had she kept her mouth closed about what she had overheard. Was God paying her back? She had so many thoughts running through her head. Will she live to see her grandmother again? Would she ever see Layla and Monique again? But the one thing that kept tugging at her heart was Layla's mom's voice earlier that morning in prayer. So, right there, Yve decided she needed a miracle to get out of this situation and so she did the only thing she could – pray. She prayed that God would allow her to get out of the situation she was in, she prayed that He would have mercy on her, she prayed for deliverance from her lifestyle. She knew that the smoking, drinking, and partying was all taking a toll on her and she vowed that if He got her out of the situation she was in, she would strive to do better. She made a lot of promises to God while she sat there in that dark cold room. She also knew that if He proved himself to her, she would prove herself to Him. Yve ended her prayer and was crying hard when someone interrupted her moment. She didn't know how long she had been sitting there but it had been at least a couple of hours since the guy had gotten off the phone with Levi.

Someone different than the first guy came in the cold dark room and like the first guy, he also wore a ski mask. Yve kept her eyes glued to his every move. He had a plate in his hand and placed it in front of her. Yve didn't think she could eat anything but after looking at the pizza and smelling it, her stomach immediately alerted her otherwise and as soon as the guy untied her hands, she grabbed the pizza and ate it as if he was quickly going to take it back.

Yve looked at the eyes of this guy and swore they looked familiar. She looked at him and watched as his eyes roamed over her body. She felt sick to her stomach at the thought of him touching her.

"Why are you doing this to me?" Yve wined and looked into the eyes of the guy that was kneeling in front of her.

"Don't talk. Just eat and give me the plate back." Yve noticed he said it calmly and without anger in his voice like the first guy who was making all the demands. Yve did as she was told and finished her pizza and gave the plate back to the guy she reasoned was not out to hurt her.

He turned around and headed back up the steps. Once again she was left alone in the cold room.

Layla, Monique, and Lyn were now riding in the same car. Nut had decided to ride with the fellas and also see in which way he could help. Layla thanked Lyn for her concern and dropped her off at home and told her she would keep her informed if she heard anything.

Layla and Monique headed back to Layla's place worried as ever. Neither spoke much in route. They really didn't know what the guys were planning and where they all were meeting at because the fellas thought the less they knew, the better off they were. Layla didn't want to hear that. She wanted to know every detail about what they had planned. Layla thought back to the conversation Yve had with Levi and Malachi in her parent's basement and screamed aloud.

"Oh my goodness!!" Layla yelled and caused Monique to jump out of her own horrible thoughts.

"What?" Monique asked Layla. "Yo, I know who may be behind Yve's kidnapping." Layla said and looked at

Monique. She immediately grabbed her cell phone and dialed Nate's number.

Luckily he picked up on the first ring. "What's up?" Nate answered.

"Nate, I think I know who is behind this?" Nate didn't want to let up that it was Layla on the line so he excused himself from out of the guys presence. They had just arrived at Malachi and Levi's warehouse off of Ritchie Marlboro Road. He walked outside and finally responded.

"Layla, how would you know something like that?" Nate questioned.

"Look, can you meet me at my place? I don't feel comfortable talking on the phone and besides, I think you need to hear this face to face." Layla explained. Monique was all ears and looking at Layla waiting for her to say who she thought was behind Yve's kidnapping.

Nate agreed to meet Layla after the guys came up with a plan. They hung up from each other and Layla filled Monique in.

Al and Nate had already dropped Nut off and told him they would definitely call him if they needed him. Prior to arriving at the warehouse, Al and Nate discussed that LaShone's homeboy had to have some information about where Yve was located so they were definitely going to go hit him up as soon as possible. The only dilemma was that this had to be done with just the two of them because there was no way to explain to the other dudes how they knew that kind of information. It would surely raise a red flag if they divulged information like that.

Back in the warehouse they were all discussing the plan. Levi and Al were to ride to meet the guy at the Warner Theatre while Malachi and Nate were to follow the guys after the drop off was made. It seemed easy enough but they knew that they would be expecting them to follow them so to go unnoticed was going to be the difficult task at hand. They decided to meet back at the warehouse tomorrow night at eight o'clock which was an hour before the drop was to be made.

The guys parted ways and Nate dropped Al off and then headed to Layla's place.

When Nate arrived, Layla and Monique was hitting a jay and sitting on pins and needles waiting to hear something about their best friend. As soon as she opened the door for Nate she started.

"Nate, I know who is behind this…" Layla said.

"How could you possibly know something like that, but anyway – spill it." Nate said trying to get to the bottom of Layla's thoughts.

"It's Sweets Babe. When Yve was first telling us about over hearing Jayden talking on the phone, he mentioned Sweets and I heard her repeat the name but I guess I didn't think it was that serious at first."

"Sweets? Yo, Layla I need to speak to you in private." Nate looked over in Monique's direction and noticed she was nodding off.

He took Layla in her room and set her down on her bed and looked straight in her eyes.

"Look, what I am about to tell you is serious and can't ever be repeated. You understand?" Nate questioned Layla.

"Yes, what it is?" Layla said trying to figure out what was about to come out of Nate's mouth.

"If what you are telling me is correct, then Sweets had something to do with me getting robbed a while ago. But listen, even though they robbed Malachi and Levi's store – they didn't get the profit." Nate studied Layla's reaction but noticed he wasn't quite making sense to her so he continued.

"Al and I followed the crew that robbed them and then took the shit they made off with."

"What? What the fuck are you telling me, Nate." Layla said and jumped up. She no longer was confused, she definitely understood what he was saying. He robbed Malachi in her eyes.

"Look, I had no idea that you and Yve knew these cats like that and that this would ever be an issue and that y'all would ever be involved. You know me better than that and know I would never put you in harm's way." Nate said staring at Layla and trying to read her thoughts.

"Okay, well you have to tell Malachi who is behind it and let him know that it wasn't about him but the guys that robbed you." Layla said and stood up from the bed and paced the little space in front of her bed.

"Layla, do you hear yourself? I am swearing you to secrecy and Al would shit bricks if he ever knew I told you something like this. What the hell do you think Malachi and Levi will say when they hear this shit? In their eyes I robbed them and have shit that belongs to them. This could easily turn into an ugly situation so you are to keep your mouth shut." Nate said and looked directly in Layla's eyes. "Shawty, I am going to take care of this shit tonight and get Yve back. That's my word. Remember we are going away after all of this is said and done. I love you Layla and I have so much set up for us so just trust me, okay?" Nate finished speaking and noticed tears coming out of Layla's eyes along with the look of fear which shook him.

"Baby, please be careful. I love you too and I swear I don't know what I would do if something was to happen to you but trust my loyalty is and always has been with you." Layla said and wiped her eyes.

She gave Nate a deep kiss and walked him to the door. "Nate, please come back to me and bring Yve home safely."

They exchanged knowing looks and Layla watched as Nate got on the elevator and locked eyes with him until the doors shut. She closed her door and looked over at Monique who witnessed the exchange and knew not to ask any questions. Monique stood up from the couch and went to Layla and they cried and hugged for what seemed like forever.

BABY G

Chapter 22

Nate left Layla's house and called Al to put a plan in motion fast. He figured that they could ride by the house they saw the guys at and hope this is where Yve was being kept. Al was ready and brought two more guys along and they were all strapped and in gear prepared for what looked like World War III. Nate gave instructions on how the plan was to be played out.

"Okay, so one of you will go to the front with me and one of you will go with Al to the rear. Let's try and keep this as clean as possible. Aim for their legs if at all possible. We just want to get Yve out of there safely." Nate said and looked at each one of them to make sure they were taking in what he was saying.

He didn't want a body on his hands but he knew that if it came down to it, it would be them before him or one of his boys. When they arrived at the house, they snuck up in a truck that was all black and resembled a truck that the jump-out-boys would be cruising in. They circled the block twice before parking a couple of houses down. Thankfully it was dark but time wasn't on their side because within the next hour or two, the sun would be rising.

They all got into position. Nate and one of the dudes were up front behind the concrete wall that separated the porch from the house and Al and the other dude was around back waiting for the signal to rush in. Nate gave the dude with him a signal to stay put and he crept to the side of the house and looked through the window to see what the numbers were looking like. To his surprise, there were only about three dudes on the first level and they were sitting on a raggedy old couch playing a game. Since there was no upstairs, he figured that Yve was in the basement and guessed that it could probably be one more down there with her but of course he had no way of being certain. He continued to the back where Al and his boy were and notified them of what they were working with. He gave them the eye signal to be on the lookout and that he was ready to move in. He made his way back to the front of the house and gave the dude there the same sign and lit the rag that was in the bottle which contained gasoline. He then threw the bottle into the window and it landed in the living room with a loud crash sound.

Yve had dosed off so the loud crashing sound immediately woke her and all she could hear were gun shots being fired. She prayed it was the police or Levi coming for her and knew this might be her only chance to escape. She tried her best to wiggle out of the ropes that had her wrists bound. Someone was coming down the steps. She couldn't make out who it was but he was dressed in all black and soon as he said her name, she knew she was safe. It was Al. She couldn't hold back the tears, she watched him cut the ropes off of her wrists and he instructed her to get up, slip her clothes on, and not make a sound. Apparently there was still a shootout going on upstairs and everything was happening so fast. Yve followed Al upstairs and out the back door. He threw her a set of keys and she took off running in the direction he pointed to.

The other dude that was with Al was in the house and was standing over two of the dudes when Al rushed back in to see what was going on and to make certain Nate was good. It turned out there was just one dude with a bullet wound in his shoulder and the other dude had a bullet hole in his head.

Al looked at them and shook his head as he headed out the front door which was wide open. As soon as he got out there, he saw Sweets standing over Nate and he immediately fired a shot in his direction but he heard Sweets gun go off the same time and he knew the unthinkable had just happened. Sweets dropped to the ground apparently hit by Al's bullet. Al ran over to Sweets and kicked the gun away from him before dropping down to check on Nate.

"Yo, come on man – we gotta get out of here. Yve is good, she's safe. Let's go!" Al pleaded with Nate.

As Al looked at his friend, he knew it was a lost cause. Blood was coming out of his mouth and when Nate tried to speak he would just cough up blood. Al couldn't help but cry for his friend. He got closer to him so he could hear what he was saying.

"Tell Layla she will always be..." Nate choked and coughed up more blood.

"I got you man, just hold on, the ambulance will be here shortly. You can tell her yourself, dawg." Al said, and yelled for Yve to call the police as she had just pulled the truck up to the house.

The other dudes jumped in and Al looked back down at Nate who was losing his fight right before Al's eyes. Police sirens could be heard in the distance.

"She will always be my Baby G." Nate weakly said before closing his eyes.

Yve was crying and rocking back and forth as she spoke to the operator on the line.

"Put him in the car cause we gotta bounce," he heard one of the boys yell.

Al, looked at his friend with closed eyes said a prayer over him and jumped in the driver's side of the car as Yve climbed to the passenger seat.

"He gone, yo." Al said aloud to no one in particular. All that could be heard was Yve screams...

"Oh, no. My god, not Layla." Yve cried for the loss of her friend and for the hurt that she knew Layla was going to be feeling.

Everyone was silent and Yve was drained. She hadn't stopped crying since Al got in the car. Al got rid of the truck and switched rides. He gave his boys dap and promised to get back at them at a later date and instructed them to stay under the radar.

Layla jumped out of her sleep and immediately start having pains in the pit of her stomach. She had such a horrible feeling and jumped up and ran to her bathroom and threw up for what seemed like forever. Layla was gagging so loud that she woke Monique up who had fell asleep on Layla's couch. She got up and went to check on her friend.

"Layla, it's five-thirty in the morning. Are you okay, Honey?" Monique asked and walked to Layla's linen closet to get her friend a washcloth.

She returned to the bathroom and wet the washcloth for Layla and helped her get up and walk back in her bedroom.

"Yeah, I guess. I was awakened out of my sleep by a sharp pain. Not only that, I can't see clearly. Something is wrong, get me the phone." Layla asked as she pointed to her cell phone which was lying on her nightstand next to her bed.

Layla dialed Nate's number and didn't get an answer. She kept calling and the phone kept ringing. Layla slid down on the floor and felt defeated. She knew something was wrong and she gave in to every bad thought imaginable and reasoned this was the why she wasn't seeing clearly and was feeling so nauseous. Layla let out a wrenching scream and Monique consoled her friend and assured her everything was okay. That Yve and Nate was both okay.

Yve was crying and didn't know how she was going to tell her friend that Nate was gone. She walked to the door of Layla's unit and knocked. Monique answered the door, saw and grabbed Yve and they held each other crying. Al walked in behind Yve. Layla came from around the corner and looked at Yve and Monique on the floor hugging and crying and then looked behind them to Al. The tears that were coming down his face was all the confirmation Layla needed. She knew her best friend and the love of her life was gone. Everything in her body told her so. She could no longer hold up her legs, she fainted right there in the middle of her living room.

Chapter 23

Layla woke up to tubes and wires connected to her chest and arms. She looked around to see where she was. She was in the hospital. She slowly remembered the events of the night before and she screamed as if she was being awakened out of a bad dream. Her mom and dad both were at her side in a moment's notice. They were apparently out in the hallway talking with the doctor. The doctor came in behind them and greeted Layla. Her mom was at her side, wiping the tears that were running down her face and whispering I love you and telling Layla everything would be okay.

"Glad you are doing well Ms. Thompson. You gave us quite a scare." The doctor said as he introduced himself to Layla and checked her vitals. "It seems you and the baby will be just fine." The doctor said and started writing results down on Layla's chart.

"Baby? What Baby." Layla asked and looked from the doctor to her mom.

"Layla, you're six weeks pregnant." Her mom told her while combing her hair back and out of her face.

"Oh my god." Was all Layla said before sobbing again. This time she cried for her unborn child because he or she would never know their father. She cried for Nate, she cried for his family, and most importantly – she cried for the emptiness she felt. A part of her was gone and she could never get him back.

"It's okay, Baby. Let it out." Her mom said while stroking Layla's face. Her dad came over with another wash cloth and handed it to her mom. Layla could barely look at her father. She felt so bad and mostly ashamed that she was now pregnant with a child who didn't have a father. She could only imagine her parent's disappointment in her. But when her eyes met her father's, they were soft and he reassured her with a smile and nod that everything would be okay.

The doctor finished up with Layla and told them that she would be discharged in another day or so. He instructed her to get plenty of rest and to not walk around much. That her first trimester was critical and that she shouldn't put a lot of strain on her unborn child.

As the doctor stepped out of the room, in came Monique and Yve with flowers and balloons in hand. Everyone greeted each other and Layla's parents excused themselves. Layla's father told her he was going to drive her mom home to get a change of clothes and bring her back to stay another day with her. Layla was grateful for her parents and suddenly felt a blanket of peace cover her.

The girls waited for Layla's parents to leave before getting emotional. They both came to both sides of Layla's bed and leaned over her. They gave her a hug and kissed her on her cheeks. Yve started first.

"Layla, I am so sorry. If he hadn't been trying..." Layla cut Yve off and hushed her.

"Yve, it's not your fault. I know that God does everything for a reason and so we won't dwell on how it happened and why. We will just try to move forward from here." Layla said and grabbed Yve's hand.

Monique and Yve couldn't believe what they were hearing. They were certain Layla would be on some warpath stuff but to their surprise, she was exceptionally calm. They all cried a little and then Layla told them about the baby. Both Yve and Monique cried even more, they cried for their girlfriend. They couldn't believe that Layla would have to raise a child by herself. It just didn't seem fair to them.

Monique changed the subject and told Layla that Carlos, Malachi, and Levi sent their well wishes. Hearing Malachi's name did something to Layla. She realized it sparked anger in her. She didn't know that he even sold drugs and lived the kind of lifestyle he lived. She started to feel bitterness towards Malachi and somewhat blame because she didn't have anyone else to blame. Layla had yet to speak to Al to find out what exactly happened that night and she wasn't honestly sure she wanted to know. But she knew she was going to have to deal with it at some point.

"Monique, have you talked to Al?" Layla asked.

"Yes, he said he will come to see you sometime today. Layla, he is really messed up behind this. I'm really concerned for him." Monique said and looked down at her friend.

"Yeah, I will talk to him." Layla said.

"I have something to tell y'all," Yve confessed. "I am moving in with Levi. He asked me this morning and after everything that has gone down, I happily said yes. I don't even know if I would've been able to sleep in my bed again. It just wouldn't have been right living there anymore. So, I plan to put the house on the market as soon as I can."

Layla didn't know how to feel about Yve's news. Her life had just shattered in her face and she wasn't sure how she was feeling about the whole situation but she told Yve that she would support her if that is what she wanted. She also told her she was welcome to come stay with her as well. Yve thanked both of the girls but was determined to be with Levi and see where it goes. She knew that Layla would need her space and she knew that Monique and Carlos was also getting more serious so she felt the best thing for her was to move in with Levi. Plus she was scarred and needed to feel that sense of protection from him.

The nurse came in and interrupted their conversation and reminded Layla that she needed to get some rest. Layla and Monique took that as a sign for them to go and to let Layla rest up. They said their goodbyes and promised to come see her tomorrow and every day after.

Layla just wanted to be left alone. She called her mother and told her she didn't have to come back and spend the night with her. She assured her she just wanted to be alone for a while and that she could come back in the morning. Layla started to think about Nate's folks and how they must be devastated. She picked up the phone to call Nate's mom. Someone picked up on the first ring. It was Nate's best friend, Chemistry. Layla hadn't realized she was even home from overseas. She was playing in a professional Women's League and had been gone for some time. Layla's heart went out to her. Nate and Chem had been friends for so long and had done everything together for as long as she could remember. She was clearly devastated. She told Layla that she had gotten married recently and that her and her wife would be staying at Nate's folk's home until the funeral. Layla told her she couldn't wait to see them both and told her she would be there as soon as she got out of the hospital. Chemistry handed Mrs. Boone the phone.

"Layla, how are you holding up?" Nate's mom asked soon as she got on the phone.

"Mama, I'm fine. The question is – how are you holding up? I'm so sorry Mrs. Boone. I'm going to miss him so much." Layla cried.

Layla wasn't sure if she should tell Nate's mom about the baby or not. She was thinking when Mr. Boone picked up a phone in another room.

"Layla, how are you Dear?" Mr. Boone asked. Layla could her Nate's mom sniffling and crying on the other end.

"Oh, Mr. Boone I am doing okay. I just can't believe he's gone. We truly will miss him. I don't know what we are going to do without him." Layla said.

"Layla, you said we." Ms. Boone said through the phone. "Layla who is we, child?" Ms. Boone asked Layla almost as if she already knew the answer.

"Oh, Mama Boone, I was just speaking for us all." Layla tried cleaning up her words.

"Layla, do you have something you need to tell us?" Mr. Boone asked.

"Ummm, yes." Layla said and cleared her throat. "Well I just found out that I'm six weeks pregnant and that..."

Layla was cut off by the sound of Mrs. Boone on the other line screaming and crying. She hadn't gotten a chance to finish her sentence but she could hear Nate's mom on the other end of the phone praising God. She could hear the happiness in her voice and that made Layla smile.

"Oh, Layla. I think you just made it a little easier for us." Mr. Boone said. "Layla, he took our son but gave us a grandchild to remember him by. You just hurry up and get better and come see us. We think we are going to have the funeral next week sometime so we need you to be strong so you can come help Bernadine with the arrangements and things." Mr. Boone said referring to his wife.

"Okay, I will. Mama Boone – you still there?" Layla cried.

"Yes, Dear. I'm still here. I'm feeling so many different emotions that I just don't know how I am going to make it."

"Mama, I will be there as soon as I am released. We will get through this together. So, keep praying and remember that God don't make mistakes." Layla said before saying her goodbyes and hanging up.

Layla put her hand on her stomach and said a silent prayer for her unborn child. She prayed that she would be a good mother and will always remind and teach her child about their father. Layla finished her prayer and decided she was going to try and get some rest. But before she knew it, Al was walking in with a big bouquet of flowers and he handed them to her.

She thanked him and she noticed a card attached. She took it off and read it.

"You Will Always Be His Baby G"

She burst out in sobs and couldn't stop. She looked at Al who also had tears coming down his face. He pulled up a chair and set directly beside Layla.

He took her hand and rubbed it gently.

"Look Layla, stop crying. It's going to be okay." Al tried telling Layla.

"What am I supposed to do without him? For that matter, how is my baby going to grow up without a father?" Layla said in between cries.

"Yo, you're pregnant?" Al asked. "Damn..." he said and shook his head.

"Layla, you need to know that you were the last thing that was on his mind when he left us. Those were his last words. He asked me to tell you that you would always be that to him. Layla, soon as you get out, I have so much to tell you and more importantly – Nate was about to make things official with you. He had just gotten a few things lined up for you and well, he would of course want you and y'all baby taken care of. So, just know that you are set. Enjoy his memory and be strong for you and my little niece or nephew. Okay?" Al tried joking a little to lighten the mood.

"Okay, I will try. Al, I need to hear everything that happened that night after y'all left me. Please don't leave anything out."

Al told Layla everything that happened against his will. But he realized she needed closure. He finished with Nate's last words which were meant for her. Layla was again in tears. She didn't know if she would ever stop crying again.

"Look Layla, I found out that Sweets is not dead. Matter of fact, he is in critical condition in this same very hospital. But, don't worry – I am going to handle him as soon as they move him out of the ICU. I can shake the guard that they got on him so I will make sure he doesn't ever walk out this hospital alive." Al whispered.

"Layla – You hear me?" Al asked.

"Yeah, I hear you." Layla smirked.

Little did Al know, Layla had stop listening after he told her that Sweets was still alive and nonetheless only steps away from her. The anger and emotions she felt wouldn't allow her to rest until Sweets was taken care of.

"Uhh, look – Al. Thanks so much for coming but I'm not feeling well and had visitors all day. I really need to get some rest." Layla tried to sound convincing.

Al thought she was acting rather strange but given everything she had been through, he ignored it and told her that he would be between his house and Nate's folk's home if she needed anything.

"Okay, thanks so much." Layla said and let Al give her a hug and kiss on her forehead before he walked out. Layla noticed it was still a little light outside and decided she would rest and wait until night hit to pay Sweets a visit.

BABY G

Chapter 24

Layla woke up with the conversation that her and Al had still on her mind. She looked at the clock and noticed it was two o'clock in the morning. She couldn't believe she had slept for hours without waking up. She first turned off her monitors so that once she unplugged the chords and tubes; it wouldn't alert the nurse's station. She winced in pain realizing that her body was so stiff from not moving around and getting out of bed for an entire day. Layla looked in the cabinet to see if her mom had brought any of her clothes to the hospital. To her surprise she hadn't but her clothes that she wore to the hospital were placed in a hospital bag and put to the side. She quickly put on her sweat suit but kept the hospital gown on under her clothes. Layla peeped out her hospital room door and noticed that the floor was so quiet and dimly lit. She was grateful that her room was near the entrance of the hall and not towards the back where the Nurse station was located. Layla snuck out undetected and headed to find the floor that ICU was located.

She picked up one of the hospital phones and an operator immediately came on. She asked where the ICU was located and hung up as soon as she got an answer. It was two floors down. She reached the floor with ICU and went to the ladies room and removed her sweat suit. Layla felt as if she was being driven and guided by another force. She couldn't explain it but she knew she couldn't rest until she was absolutely certain Sweets was taken care of. She waited for someone to open the door to the ICU and walked right in as soon as it opened. It was set up similar to an Emergency room with beds and curtains lined all around and the nurse's station was sitting in the middle of the floor. Thankfully no one was at the desk but it seems as if everyone was doing something and she was so far going undetected.

"Code Blue!" Layla heard a nurse yell and watched as everyone scrambled to a patient's bedside.

Layla slipped into a unit and walked from unit to unit until she came upon Mr. Jamal aka Sweets Nichols himself. She starred at him with tears in her eyes. She couldn't believe she was standing in front of Nate's killer. She cut off his heart machine and waited to see if that would alert anyone. She noticed it didn't so she quickly moved on. She grabbed the pillow from behind his head and put it over his face. He was oblivious of what was going on seeing as though he was unconscious. She bent down and put the pillow over his face. He squirmed a little and she held the pillow down tighter while whispering in his ear.

"You are nothing but a snake and you are now getting exactly what your punk ass deserves."

She looked down and noticed his hands was cuffed which explained why there wasn't an officer around. She noticed he had stop moving completely and took the pillow off of his face. His face was almost a bluish-purple color but was coming back to its regular color. She spit on his face and turned the machine back on as she walked back out and through other patients spaces while being undetected back out to the hallway.

She went back in the ladies room and could hear a nurse scream, "Code Blue Mr. Nichols."

Layla was satisfied and returned to her room undetected. She lay in her bed and spoke aloud to Nate as if he was in the room.

"Baby, we will miss you more than you know. Now you can rest – your Baby G has your back. Love you with all my heart."

Layla put her hands behind her head and drifted to sleep with a satisfied grin on her face.

PART II

COMING SOON!

BABY G

ABOUT THE AUTHOR

M. Lakeya Edwards currently resides in Springdale, Maryland and is a Management and Program Analyst for the United States Government. She is also the CEO of Baby G Entertainment & Publishing. Ms. Edwards is also the mother of one son and is hard at work on her next novel.

You can email her at:

Lakeya@BabyGLLC.com

or visit her at

www.BabyGLLC.com

and

www.facebook.com/BabyGLLC

You can also follow her on twitter

to stay abreast of all of her literary work

@KeyaSassyWriter.